ISBN: 9781704224107

Independently published

Available on Amazon.co.uk

After '*Nori,*'and '*My classic boat,*' '*Edward*' is my third book which tells the story of Edward, an excellent artist and a nurse, who was so in love with his own paintings, he was reluctant to sell them!

Edward is a dramatization where a muse had become his love in reality. Despite his wife's awareness, she remained calm and forgiving for him to lead a blissful life in harmony.

I totally disclaim all the names mentioned in the book to be the exact individuals that come into mind.

I thank David Rollason (artist), *at the Pens of Erdington*, for the page design and book cover.

Edward…

CHAPTER 1

It was the midst of December 1969, the weather wasn't very warm outside, but the spirit of Christmas was around to warm the hearts. The post office at Stockland Green was busy with occasional long queues as people had already started posting their greetings to loved ones abroad and inland. The small bunch of people arriving was always jovial. They smiled, joked, with instant hilarity.

At the other end of the counter, two attractive young girls wearing glittering tinsels that matched the colour of their hair were dishing out stamps, placing them on already sealed envelopes and packages. Always chatty to customers, well known to them it seemed, as the community at Stockland Green was small then. One of the girls had the coiffure of Judith Durham, the lead singer of the Seekers. The other was a likely image of Dusty Springfield, famous for her song 'When I say I love you'.

There were some hints of shyness in the girls' appearances but their jaunty talks showed otherwise. Nothing could disguise the fact that those girls were flirty, especially when a certain young handsome lad coiffured with the prevalent *Beatles'* styles of the day stood in front of them. He stood by the cashier where *Judith Durham* look alike was serving. He gave her a Christmas Card. She returned the compliment with another Card as she blushed and froze instantly. Although distraught, she continued serving. Her colleague sat next to her at the counter was equally intrigued. She looked at them at the corner of her eyes, while serving her own customers, said nothing. They had both seen him before.

It was five years ago Edward arrived in Erdington from Soweto to seek his fortune. He was an 18 years old then, with light skin colour that could easily be mistaken for a dark Englishman. The two girls at the counter had always fascinated him. He had developed a deep secret love for one of them, but too shy to reveal it to her, as a certain rebuke from her could spell disaster for the fantasy he cherished daily. Being good at painting and doing tapestry work in Africa, he had drawn her pictures from memory on blank sheets of paper that could be seen on the wall of his room. The rather comely, pretty face with the blond fringe on the forehead in the picture was more than a muse. Enough inspiration was invoked where lines of poetry were written to compliment the pictures he drawn. Although he couldn't have her physical self, he knew the recess of his room was there for her. If only he could conjure her presence through some form of subtleties to be in his room, he would thank God more than a thousand times!

He didn't know the girl's name yet the Christmas Card was written and given. Apart from the greetings, the iconic image of the Virgin Mary was typical for a card. He wrote a few lines of his own to show the spiritual virtues of the seasonal greetings, and a date with her, which he diligently wrote with shaky hands showing a certain form of shyness of his own. He desperately wanted to meet her by the number 11 Bus stop when she finished work that evening.

He made the bold and hopeful attempt to be there on time. Not many people were waiting for the bus in front of the Post Office, and he had pushed his appearance to the limit. Apart from being close-shaved, his exotic perfumed was enough to mesmerize any desperate soul into submission. There were more chances to exchange a few words with her then, even going further by jumping into the bus with her, bearing towards Erdington High Street.

Her first name was Julie when the card was opened, with a 'crossed' kiss by her name, enough to signify 'Love'. The similar serene image on the card she received was a larger version of Virgin Mary, excel in beauty itself, that easily echoed his muse.

It was 6 p.m. Friday, the number 11 red Bus had arrived, Edward waited for a while. Julie came out quickly after somebody closed the Post Office door behind her. Edward started to blush, with increased heartbeats. She gave him a quiet smile, which he returned with an enthused expression that shined in his eyes.

They both sat side by side, while the bus moved along. They looked at each other, still smiling, not knowing who will break the ice first, but her strong scent of Lilly of the Valley mingled with his own brand, was heavenly. They looked at each other again, still smiling, but she made the first move:

'Shall we stop in Erdington?'

'Oh Yes,' he replied.

They both got down in Erdington by the roundabout. They walked up the High Streets towards Edwards Edwards, a coffee shop, a more likely spot for them 'to get to know each other better.'

'Shall we go for a coffee?' asked Edward.

Julie nodded with a smile. They both got inside, decided to park on a single table for two. Edward went to get the coffee and cakes. He gently placed what he brought on the table and sat down opposite her, persistently admiring her good looks, while sipping his coffee, and having a quick nibble at his cake. Julie remained calm and speechless, perhaps shocked by his kind attention. She got no room to manoeuvre it appeared with his repeated gaze that seemingly looked through her. She had to avert that gaze while taking a bite at the cake, and looked away.

'Nice cake isn't it?' asked Edward.

'Yes very tasty. Did you bake it, since it is your shop!' asked a smiling Julie with a hint of banter.

'No Julie it isn't my shop, although we carried the same name,' replied Edward smiling.

He noticed a little ring on her finger, kept looking at it. He hoped she wasn't married, but hesitant to ask. She soon realized his problem by making it easy for him, and said:

'No Edward I am not married. What about you? Which country are you from? Do you like it here?'

Edward wasn't fluent in English, yet tried to answer all her questions. He found out that she was about the same age, was glad that she was single, and seemed willing to get to know him.

'I left South Africa a few years ago, I live in a flat in Stockland Green, but I missed home dearly. No work in Soweto, I work at the sandwich factory here since I arrived. My English is not very good. They told me I must learn the English ways. I started night school at Sutton College to study English, because I want to be a Nurse. Do you live local?'

She had finished her last piece of cake, but he ate only half of his, through the excitement of knowing her. She knew she had a few admirers, Edward wasn't the least. She started to feel more relaxed now to talk about how she had worked at the post office a few months ago, that she lived in Stetchford with her mum and dad. They could have stayed longer talking but it was getting late, and the shop was closing. Edward made a move for a future engagement. He made another bold attempt to ask:

'Shall we meet tomorrow since you are off half day?'

Julie seemed thoughtful but pleasant.

'I can't over the weekend. But come to the post office tomorrow, I shall let you know.'

With that said they got up to hit the road. Edward was hopeful. Julie had all night to decide what to do. A sudden anxiety matched by positive alacrity started to build up, everything looked promising for Edward. They walked towards the Bus stop heading for Stetchford. A bus was already waiting. Before she jumped inside she tenderly looked at him with a smile, and gave him a peck on the cheek. Edward nearly swooned. He waved to Julie again and again until the bus disappeared amidst the bright lights of the street decorations. He would have more than a sweet dream tonight: His muse had eventually materialised into a living work of art!

CHAPTER 2

Edward arrived at the post office the next day before dinner time. The long queue was moving fast carrying Edward with it. He appeared in front of her in no time. The greetings with smiles were apparent. Another card from her was dished out quickly with a message inside. The queue behind was amazed by the quick service, but Edward had 'come, he saw and had conquered.' He couldn't wait to open the card, which read 'since it was Christmas week on Monday, and I am off half day, shall we meet by the bus stop at 1 p.m.?' He could feel his heart beating with joy and excitement. It seemed like a reply from Venus herself!

Saturday, and Sunday went quickly. Edward made sure he was off half day too. He arrived at the bus stop as planned. Julie was already there, and Edward gave her a kiss on the cheek as they jumped on the bus.

The pavement in Erdington was iced up from the snow left behind the day before. It started to snow again. They decided to head for the Bull Ring in town, where no doubt there would be better things to feast the eyes on, and to cement their newly found love for each other.

The Bull Ring was fully alive with distinctive sounds of Christmas Carols when they arrived. It was another world from the one they left outside: Sequential flashing lights flickering different hues hanging on Christmas trees, and ceilings: the roof of heaven was twinkling above. The whole scene was transformed into some vast indoor galaxies, with cheerful customers went in and out of shops with more Carols songs in the background. But he kept looking at her, and she returned that gaze, smiling. They had started to hold hands now!

The Gino restaurant was in full view. Since it was dinner time they decided to go for a meal. They sat on a single table for two as before and ordered stakes menu. The menu arrived by a waiter, amidst their conversation.

'So do you celebrate Christmas like here in South Africa? What is your mother tongue?' asked Julie.

'We do celebrate Christmas, but not as great as here though. We talk Africans and French, but we have to learn English at schools. No we don't paint our faces and dance around big pots on fire with spears in our hands. But we enjoyed the outdoor lives.'

'Oh you make me laugh, excuse me!' sniggered Julie, and continued smiling, as it was intentional for Edward to go for a crack as a testing ground for Julie to respond. But Julie got the vague perceptions of visualising him doing just what he said. She wasn't aware of the communal distinction and the improved lifestyles of the country. She regretted the fact of stereotyping people in her thoughts! But she suddenly realised that she had to accept Edward as he was. She admired his good looks, and wanted to learn more about his church affiliation:

'I am not that religious, what about you? Because by sending similar cards to each other we look like missionary folks preparing to enter the religious orders..!'

'You make me laugh now!' said Edward.

Julie couldn't care about races or religion. As far as she was concerned, Edward was in England now not Africa. She wanted to be simple in her language and helped him instead, as she noticed for herself how he struggled to get his words right at times.

'So you lived in Stockland Green on your own? You got any hobby?' she asked.

'Yes I live in a small room by myself. I like drawing, I like football, and watching the telly, but I can't rent one, my front door is too small. I want a big telly you see.'

'You better get one because the World Cup is coming in June next year. Everybody is talking about Brazil and the famous player Pelé.'

'I will have to get one desperately. If I struggle to get it through the front door, I will have to use the back passage I think,' replied Edward.

'What! Oh my God!' Julie chuckled, 'I think you definitely must learn more English ways Edward!'

'Why you laugh so much? Have I said something wrong?' Edward was intrigued but pleasant.

'I was laughing because you must have translated your French or African words literally which are rude in English. Do you mean going through the backdoor?'

'This is what I mean Julie, sorry about that. I must be careful what I say in the future.'

'You needn't have to feel sorry Edward, we must all learn from each other.'

'Thanks for being very understanding, Julie. The meal was nice. Shall I pay for it and move on?'

'The meal was nice indeed. I will pay half. And I must go home too. It's getting late.'

They got up, and soon found themselves in the precincts, joining the cheering ambience again. They walked along a gift shop containing state of the art, designer handbags. Still holding her hand, they went inside. He decided to buy her one from the handful collections which she had admired too. Although it was a bit much for his pocket, it was worthwhile he reckoned since it was a Christmas gift.

'No, you shouldn't Edward, it's too expensive,' said Julie.

'My dear it's a gift, a token of my love for you for Christmas.'

'Do you mean your love is only for Christmas, what about after Christmas then?' replied Julie with a lingering smile.

'You will always be my love, today, tomorrow or the next day,' said Edward with glittering eyes, while giving her the wrapped present and a peck on the cheek.

They caught the bus for Erdington. Julie had to get her own bus nearby when they reached. A queue was there at the number 11 Bus Stop, and they waited at the rear in semi darkness. But they couldn't escape the occasional bright lights of the passing cars, reflected their shadows on the shop's white wall opposite: The shady image projected was indeed a memorable Hollywood style embrace, matched by a long warm kiss!

Julie arrived home late. Phil, her dad was concerned. He had noticed her daughter's distinct euphoria lately which was far from the exuberance of the seasonal cheer, but was hesitant to question her tardiness. He knew that John, Julie's boyfriend, normally arrived back with her when late, but she came through the door on her own. The fact that Julie was alone with something that looked like a present he presumed that she went out with her workmates. But Julie's mum, Heather, wasn't shy to ask:

'I haven't seen John lately. Is he OK? You would have thought he would be here, since it is Christmas. He must have disappeared for not giving you a present!'

Julie put her wintry coat away, and settled down on the settee, started unwrapping the present, eager to show what she had. She tried to avoid talking about John. She had finished with him, didn't tell her mum and dad. They were surprised to see the gift, and wondered why she had to buy such an expensive item. But they had their reservations.

'Did you buy it for yourself or is it a gift from your friends?' asked Phil intrigued.

'It's neither. Somebody very nice bought me this. He is the new man in my life now. He isn't English though. He is from Soweto in Africa, and lives in Erdington,' said a relaxed Julie.

Julie was thrilled to talk about Edward. Her mum and dad just listened, with a pensive mood. They knew Julie and John had been going out for nearly a year. John seemed to be a pleasant fellow, well- mannered, and expected some good news from them such as going further than being 'good friends'. It wouldn't be happening now. Julie felt the pain about the breaking up too, but kept it to herself as she already had crush on Edward to keep herself occupied.

'What lead to the break up then? Was it amicable?' asked Phil reluctantly.'

'We both agree to break it. He wanted me to be converted to the Mormons before we went on further. I know the religion got stringent rules. He said his members won't accept me unless I become one of them. So we leave it to that, as he will be treated with contempt if we carry on with me not converted. He called it a day, and I said no problem.'

'So long as you know what you are doing Julie, that you seemed to be happier than before with your new fellow, get on with your life. You are old enough to be responsible,' said Heather.

'Thanks mum you understand… what do you think dad?'

'I totally agree with your mum Julie. Let's celebrate the new relationship, bring a beer for me,' said a happy Phil.

Both parents made no comments about Edward's African origin. Since their daughter was attractive, they thought it was just a passing phase among the many admirers in her repertoire, and that Christmas gone, her dreams would no doubt be nuanced by another epiphany of reality. Hoping she would be able to be more in touch with herself.

Meanwhile Edward never missed a day to come to the post office just to see her. They went to the usual coffee shop at times for a chat before she headed home. Friday was Christmas Eve, she had finished half a day. They both went to Town again for a long walk, and a meal, since they wouldn't see each other because Julie was having her own friends and family around. But she could be generous in offering her own token of appreciation to keep her love alive. Window shopping at the H Samuel's jewellery shop in town was mesmerizing. She noticed Edward was looking at a wall clock, because he got none at the moment. They both went inside. It was Julie's turn now to buy him a present.

Christmas went quickly, and the New Year too was far away now, Edward was glad he was successful at the interview for a student nurse job at Highcroft Hospital. He had to move to the Hospital accommodation where there were free board and lodging, and he didn't spend much time to move there. He was looking forward to invite Julie to his new room, hopeful she would accept now, because she had turned down all his previous offers.

CHAPTER 3

June 1970 had arrived. World Cup fever drove people nuts. Television rental shops were busy, as people could watch football in colour now. But Edward didn't have to rent one, as there was a big one in the communal lounge next to his room. He had settled down nicely, bringing all Julie's drawings, including her own picture, which he placed on his wall as previously, and not forgetting the wall clock Julie gave him hanging by his bed.

It was Saturday. At last Julie had accepted to visit him in his room after work. Edward went to fetch her by the Bus Stop. They walked back to his room which wasn't far off Slade Road.

Edward opened his room door and asked Julie to make herself at home, while he went out to bring some tea. He returned with the tea, and placed them on his table. Julie was sitting on his bed, admiring the pictures on the wall. She cast a cursory glance at him:

'It's very cosy here,' she said, feeling the soft bed underneath her. 'Nice room too, Edward. The drawings on the wall are supposed to be me? Very interesting, what a talent, did you draw them yourself?'

'I did indeed,' said Edward, looking at his record player. 'Let's have some music, shall we?' said Edward picking a record from Andy Williams' albums and placed it on the disk player.

The record went softly spinning away, while they finished their cups of tea. Edward sat close to her on the bed, as he could feel his both hands gently reaching out her warm waist, drawing her close to him. The tune on the track was 'Wise men say only fools rush in.' But Julie, far from ready 'to rush in,' used the clock as a distracting technique to avert his glistening eyes that kept staring at her with a passion. Not to be overtly rude, she said something sensible:

'Oh Edward that clock on the wall is too low, let me place it a little higher for you, I am a bit taller than you.'

'OK Julie as you please. It had just stopped at 4 p.m. anyway. I need to buy another battery.'

Julie got up to move it higher onto another hook above. Edward was watching her while remained seated on the bed, persistently admiring her. When she finished, in front of him she stood. He felt an irresistible urge to hold her by the waist again and pulled her onto his lap, and they both ended up lying on the bed. He started kissing her most tenderly. She knew that she was under his spell now, too late to save her modesty. But deep inside, felt safe, because Edward wasn't the type to engage in the seedy side of life. He was more of a gentlemanly kind, respected and worshipped women with a pastoral devotion akin to the tragi-comedian middle age era, where women were regarded as emotional characters and chaste. Being a keen painter, and always harbouring unrealistic fantasies of a romantic kind, he was careful not to transgress the boundaries of human dignity. But he had his urges which were natural and sensual, that could easily get out of hand, and led him somewhere he had never been before! Being new to the English ways of life, the free love of the flower power hadn't influenced him yet. He certainly believed in the sanctity of marriage, and, that premarital love violated the conventional standard of human worth. It was a value inherited from his African life style, and indoctrinated by his mother, that sexual love had to be consummated with eventual marriage.

Meanwhile, the warm emotional kissing continued in bed, the waiting game for wanting to be loved continued for Julie. Underneath him she could feel his body quivering, although both remained fully clothed. The sudden cheering crowd from the television set next door had deadened the music in his room. It was Pelé scoring a goal. But Edward hadn't scored his yet, only woke up from his unfulfilled amorous venture and reverie. Julie's net was open Edward only had to kick the ball in, but missed! Unable to understand the depth of his feelings, the waiting game seemed to be over for Julie. She had been through a frustrating moment, where emotional love had taken over the sensual, where spiritual love maintained its religious significance. She realised Edward's innocence in his love for her. She had wished she was more forthright to cross the line of her female mores of modesty in telling Edward 'to get on with it, I haven't got all night you know!'

'I have never been kissed so much like that before darling Edward, but I have to go home now. Surely it's later than that stopping clock there. Will you accompany me home, my parents would like to meet with you? They have already seen us both together,' said Julie, sitting on the bed trying to prop herself up.

'May I ask where, hiding somewhere out of sight I suppose, perhaps in Erdington?'

'Yes somewhere there. Have no fear. They like you and your career as a nurse,'

'In this case I come with you. Since I love you so much, and I am sure we will get on well….shall we get engaged before next Christmas?' said Edward, kneeling in front of her placing both his arms on her knees, looking at her.

'What! Oh you are so kind Edward, yes we shall.'

Edward and Julie caught the bus for Stetchford. Her mum and dad were waiting to welcome them, but with a lukewarm reception that Julie could tell from the look in their eyes, they weren't their usual selves. Certainly it had nothing to do with Edward's appearance. They had both seen him before and seemed to like him. But the struggle with their thoughts was apparent. However, the welcoming gestures never went undiminished. Edward was asked to sit down with them. They momentarily disguised their inward feelings, and wanted to know more about him. Phil was having his beer as usual, while tea and cakes were brought by Heather.

'So your name is Edward, that's a nice name. I came across many Edwards in Cape Town, while working in the oil refinery, before I came back to England.'

'Glad to know you worked in South Africa Mr. Phil. What made you come back here then?'

'My contract expired, but I like Cape Town. What made you come here at such a young age then?'

'He came to England because of me, dad,' said Julie with a smile.

'Yes looking for problem!' replied Heather with a banter.

'What problem mum? We both intend to be engaged before next Christmas you know!' said a jubilant Julie.

There was a cough and a choke, it was Phil.

'Are you OK dad?' said Julie.

'Yes what I was going to say was: that I am happy for you both. Wish you good luck,' said Phil, still red in the face after the choking spell.

'Thanks Mr. Phil,' said Edward.

Edward decided to leave after a while, and Julie went to see him off at the bus stop. He was glad he had met both Julie's parent. Despite the fact that he was accepted, he was deeply intrigued but ambiguous about their presence. It must be his first impression of them he thought. He never stopped thinking about life changes, and his oncoming proposal to Julie while travelling back on the bus. September would be the date he reckoned when he would have enough savings to buy her a ring.

After dropping Edward, Julie arrived home to join her mum and dad on the settee. Phil and Heather maintained their silence, nuanced by a dead pan feature, just sat there watching the television with a blank vision, following nothing! Difficult to connect with Julie's current sparks of joy, not knowing either who would drop the bombshell first. A bombshell indeed: where the arrow of reality could penetrate the fantasy of a dream to hurt vulnerable victims. Heather decided to proceed first:

'John came you know. He was full of apology, and in tears for leaving you. He went to America for four months to follow his venture with the Mormons. But he was disillusioned with the whole thing. He looks like a broken man. He wants to make up with you.'

Julie's face changed. She could feel a sudden rush of blood to her head, enough to make her faint. She paused, after a while she regained her composure.

'Why did you let him in? You know I have finished with him. I am with Edward now, I don't want to see John anymore,' said Julie.

'We had to let him in Julie. We haven't seen him for a long time. It's not fair,' said Heather.

'He left me without even saying good bye, and no news from him. What do you expect me to do?' said Julie very upset.

'I understand that Julie. I know it would be difficult for you to accept him back, but try to be friends at least. Since we know him and his family well, and he had realised his mistake, you should forgive him. I think he says he is coming here to see you tomorrow,' said Phil.

'He can come if he wants to but I shall lock myself in my room. I don't want to see him, or forgive him,' said Julie, still upset, as she went to her room upstairs.

Julie had something else to think about now. She couldn't go out and hide the next day, since Edward too was working a long day that Sunday. Not anywhere to go it seemed, but the confine of her room to contend with. She had a long thought about John, who used to love her to bits, until he joined the Mormons, who she surmised apart from the spiritual well-being it promised, it was a subculture that implied submission with rigid rules to comply with.

Julie didn't sleep well on the night. She kept thinking how would she behave when she saw John? She had known him since childhood, her distant cousin on her mother's side. But they only started going out less than a year ago. She couldn't think what made him leave her. She couldn't imagine that his religion seemed to have come first. Before he left, she noticed there was no love for her in his eyes, just a blank stare like looking at a piece of furniture. There were no feelings, no regrets or remorse only the look of a stranger looking at another stranger. Now that he was coming, ready to pour down tears to rekindle the demise of the old relationship, how would she respond? She had watched stage drama before with him at the Birmingham Repertory Theatre. She remembered some disturbed scene, which affected him as he fainted, she hoped not to expect similar scene likely to draw Julie's sympathy. He could be dramatic, easily feigned psychological symptoms to attract attention. His weak character had certainly played a part to make him susceptible to psychological indoctrination, and went as far as America to join the cult there!

Before Julie started another relationship, she made sure John wouldn't be back. America is a big place, and John would probably have a lot to do there. His mum Margaret, who was living with her partner, Jill, at Castle Bromwich, didn't know either where he was. She had written several letters, tried to contact him by phone, still no response. But she was shocked with disbelief when he returned to knock at the door. Julie was going out strong with Edward then.

As Julie was twisting and turning in bed, she could still remember her good times with John. When he loved her for the first time, he promised to marry her with the ring he bought her. She still wore it in her finger. She used to go and see auntie Maggie with him, who liked her very much too, and was prepared to accept them living with her after marriage. But she noticed a sudden change in him after joining the religious group. The warmth, care and attention weren't there for her, and he seemed more interested in that religion. Now Edward was doing what John did initially, except that Edward was playing the waiting game, John had already followed his natural instinct. Upon this balancing act, Julie weighed both men, where she had to make a choice in the end.

It was dinner time Sunday. John arrived with a bunch of roses and large bar of chocolate. Julie was still in bed. Her mum and dad were having dinner. There was enough dinner for him to sit down with them, but Julie was still in her room upstairs. She could hear them downstairs, but wished that John could go away. Suddenly she realised there was no way she could avoid seeing him. She would have to tell him in all honesty how circumstances had changed now, that he had to get used to changes.

John sat down at the table with them, having something to eat, while Phil and Heather were finishing their dinner. They both went in the kitchen, deliberately colluded to leave John alone. They came back to say:

'How is Maggie then, did you tell her we are coming to see her?' asked Phil.

'No. But she is at home all day today. How is Julie, where is she?' asked John.

'She is in her room somewhere. We will leave you to it. Come on Heather let's go.'

They both got into the car and drove off, leaving John alone to finish his dinner. They wanted John and Julie to get back together. They noticed how John was a changed man after he realised his mistakes. He appeared like a more matured individual that seemingly de-radicalised, ready to take up responsibility on the world stage. They didn't dislike Edward though, although they knew something of his background. Phil knew about the African way of life, as he used to work there, that tribal villages varied from one another. Edward was a nice fellow no doubt, but the fact that his entry visa had to be renewed yearly, they didn't want Julie to suffer too if the Home Office didn't renew it. All these thoughts were travelling with them as they drove to see Margaret.

Meanwhile the silence at home was phenomenal. Julie thought that they had all gone, and was left on her own. She came downstairs in her dressing gown half undone for a drink. John was by the stairs, waiting with the bunch of flower and chocolate when he heard her coming down. He said:

'Hello Julie.'

There was no reply. Julie looked at him, shocked with what he brought her, ignored his goodwill advances, and went straight to the kitchen. He followed her there, and kneeled down with the flower and chocolate still in his hands. She looked at him again. She noticed more warmth in his eyes, more radiance in his feature now, than on the day he left her.

He got up, as she went pass by him with her drink, making her way to the table. She could smell the aroma emanating from the roses. It was reminiscent of the first date with him, and just as intoxicating as his good looks, zooming all over her. Her kind nature didn't dictate rudeness, but a more placid, spiritual kind ready to forgive. She had to answer him now knowing the alternative was brashness, which didn't become of her.

'I thought we had both finished. Why did you come back,' said Julie. John followed her and sat opposite her at the table.

'I came back for you Julie, you know I will. I changed my mind about many things before, now it is the Mormons,' said John.

'I thought you've gone forever, no news from you. Your mum and I wrote to you many times.'

'I thought so too that I won't be coming back. I wasn't myself when I went. It was a real struggle to get back here. Apart from being friendly, the friendships in the camp went too far I reckoned. I was dying to get out. But I finally did, because I did a pretend blackout one day, they fell for it, when they thought I was dying. I was sent to hospital. I ran away from there.'

'You must be lucky to get out, as I told you before they persecute deserters. Are you sure they won't be looking for you here?'

'No way Julie, I know better now. What about you? What have you been doing with yourself? I could still see my ring in that finger. And I still love you!

'Do you really, after leaving me for so long?' said Julie not amused.

'I do really. Please understand me Julie. It was like a prison, no contact with the outside world there. I desperately wanted to write to you especially, to tell you about the situation I was.'

Julie became thoughtful didn't know how to respond. She was in a quandary too. In all honesty she had to tell him about Edward. It was up to John now to react in this trio forming, in this triangle of forces, where the three of them, Edward, John, and Julie, had to struggle to either stabilise or fall. But she knew too the penchant for John had been rekindled by degrees in his presence.

'And I was left alone here, not knowing what to do. I thought I lost you. Somebody told me he loved me in Stockland Green where I worked. I thought he was bluffing. I started to fall for him. We went out together since last Christmas. He hasn't loved me yet, you must believe me. He would only love me once we are engaged before this Christmas. Edward is a very respectable fellow. He is kind and caring, and is from Africa. Don't think I dislike you John, you will still be my John.'

John was listening patiently with a touch of jealousy perhaps coupled with a sense of loss. His feature expressed sadness, as his eyes started to glitter, reacting to the tears formed. He looked at her pretty face with feelings of despair while the aroma from the roses in the front persistently bombarding them. He suddenly realized he had lost her. But deep inside, he was hopeful because Julie still wore his ring. She could be driven off course by the other guy Edward, through the deep love he had for her. He had to apologise first and regret the fact that he left her.

'Oh Julie how could you? I felt sorry I left you. But you know that I always come back for you. As for me I can say there was no other woman involved apart from the cult I joined, but for you, another man is involved. I do regret indeed. Please Julie don't leave me,' said John sadly.

He held her hand with the ring finger on the opposite side of the table, and looked at her in the eye. They both looked at each other giving an expression that they wanted to engage badly in both emotional and physical with a renewed chemistry. He got up from his seat to join her on the opposite side of the table. She got up in turn to meet his open arms. She knew she was made to feel guilty because of her quick move to find somebody else, forgotten all about him. But now that he was embracing her with voracious kisses on her mouth and neck, she could feel his body, as her dressing gown gave way: he could touch her nakedness!

They both went upstairs to her room. What took place was the wildest love making they ever had. John made up for lost time, and Julie made up for the frustrating moment of titillation with Edward.

They stayed in bed for hours, sticking to each other like glue. They finally decided to get up and get dressed. It was tea time. Phil and Heather would be back soon.

Julie and John had made it up as her parent expected. How was she going to get the other man, Edward, out of her life was still bothering her. She had grown a certain liking for him. And he worshiped her like a deity. She didn't want to be dishonest with him. She had to tell him the truth, because she admired him for doing nursing, a job she hoped to embark one day. But how was she going to break the news to him? Breaking up could be very sad. She would have to remain as friends. If he would accept it now was a different matter!

Julie became thoughtful while sitting at the table. John sensed her problem. He was convinced that Julie still loved him, and that Julie had chosen him instead of Edward. To bring some hope in his rather unclear mind, he decided to pop the question now before it was too late. He kneeled down again in front of her holding a single rose this time:

'Will you marry me darling Julie?' he asked.

'Yes my love,' she replied with a smile, cupping his face with both hands. 'But wait till next Christmas my dear in case you cleared off again. Have you got a job yet darling?'

'They accepted me back as an Activity Organiser at Highcroft, to organise patients' daily activity. No darling, I will never leave you again I promise.'

Julie was pleased to hear that he got his job back at the Hospital. She hadn't mentioned about Edward's job as a nurse there yet. She was hopeful that Edward didn't get to know him before she told him herself. They both started kissing again, but stopped when they heard the key in the door. They sat down by each other at the table, calm and innocent.

'Nice to see you both you look so relaxed and smiley. What's happened?' asked Phil.

'We are going to be married before Christmas dad,' said a jubilant Julie.

'We are so pleased for you both,' said Heather and Phil, giving them a kiss and a hug.'

'Let's drink to the occasion,' said a smiling Phil, 'I must break the news to Maggie.'

They all sat down at the table. While having their tea, Maggie turned up at the door. It was a celebration indeed!

CHAPTER 4

Edward was busy working at the hospital over the week end. He only managed to get to the post office hoping to say a quick hello the next day. But Julie wasn't there as she didn't turn up for work. It seemed that she had to get over the amorous acts of the day before, and thinking of how to tell Edward the change in circumstances! Her working colleague, Jane, responded with her usual smile to tell Edward that she was sick. The next day too she didn't turn up. Edward was thinking of going to see her at home, but changed his mind as he didn't want to bother her too much. Edward suspected there was something fishy when he met her at the bus stop the following day Wednesday, because Julie wasn't her usual self. She was thoughtful, with responses rather lukewarm instead of her usual enthusiasm. She said:

'Sorry Edward I don't feel well. I couldn't stop in Erdington either. I have to go home.'

'Is there anything wrong Julie?'

'Nothing, I am just tired. I see you over the week end.'

'I won't be here next week end Julie. I am on an assignment from the Hospital with other staff, to take patients out on holiday by Coach to Great Yarmouth for a week.'

'Oh lucky for some, our sub post office is closing you know.'

'When, Julie when? I hope it isn't tomorrow?'

'Fairly soon, and I have to find another job. Sorry I have to go Edward, my bus is here. Give me a ring later.'

Edward gave her a peck on the cheek and off she went, leaving him watching the bus disappeared on Reservoir

Road. He wasn't happy with how things had turned out for Julie. He surely would miss her behind the counter. Still the other problem that would decide their fate hadn't reached him yet! He phoned her when he reached home. She told him she couldn't see him on Thursday either. Edward was disappointed but kept his cool.

Friday had arrived, the Coach left the Hospital ground for Great Yarmouth. The coach was half full, despite the three staff including Edward, and surprisingly the Activity Organiser John were among them! The therapeutic environment had to be maintained with staff introducing themselves to one another. Among the few 'Edwards' on the coach, 'Johns' were just as common. Whether John remembered his rival by the name Edward, was difficult to envisage. John could hardly be bothered after all because Julie would be his, he was confident.

The bunch of institutional patients on the coach was rowdy, as they displayed individual weirdness characterised by their mental derangement. Some laughed aloud for no reasons apparent, some gesturing to unseen personnel, and some just sat there with eyes closed unwilling to engage.

There was a particular well - built individual with a smiling face sat by the window. He had an uncanny resemblance to the known actor Telly Savalas, Kojac. All he could say repeatedly when under stress was: 'my mother is concerned,' and started to kiss the glass window of the coach or anything, now and again. He also seemed to respond to any name he heard to be his own. Well, let's called him 'Charlie.'

Another individual called 'John,' who kept repeating the same sentence, 'What did you do to that Doreen?' Sitting next to him was Ted, who was so conditioned to the word

Doreen that he responded whenever he heard 'her name' being mentioned by saying: 'I *fog* her!'

With all the drama enfolded, Edward was watching those deranged individuals travelling closely. Sitting by him was a middle age nurse called Shaun, who was also a priest. Edward wondered what was in God's mind when He made people different if we are all considered equal. Being the only student, looking for a positive answer, Shaun replied:

'Equal only in the eyes of the Lord, lad, we all see something different to make us realise and think how we can improve life.'

'If it was God's will to cause the difference, some of us are certainly worst off, living in pain with dysfunctionality to go with!'

'The good Lord never wanted it that way lad. It is man's own doing in this troublesome world.'

'So mankind is the cause. What can God do about it?'

'God can do nothing lad. Being the cause of it, man has to redress the suffering himself, by finding ways in line of treatments.'

Shaun didn't want to engage in a long drawn argument on religious matters. He knew it would be like 'a chicken and egg' riddle. They both went quiet for a while, observing the occupants in the coach and the view outside. He changed subject to ask Edward:

'How is life in Africa then? Are you happy here?'

'Life is not so good in Africa. This is why I came here. I miss mum. Hoping to go and see her during my next holiday.'

'Have you got friends or a girlfriend here perhaps?'

'I've got a girlfriend. She works at the post office.'

'Does she work at Stockland Green?'

'Yes she does. I believe the post office is closing soon.'

'So I believe. They are trying to close some sub post offices in Erdington. There are two nice girls working there, which one is yours?'

'Oh that's a secret,' said Edward smiling.

While they were chatting away, the bus reached a Service Station where they had to stop for a short break and to use the toilets facilities. All patients were closely watched in case they strayed when they got down from the coach. In a single file they walked inside the Service Station. Edward and Shaun went with a few to assist them with the toilets.

'Charlie' was among the few, and he couldn't wait in the bunch. He strayed once in the toilets area, and started kissing the toilet walls and doors. He went to the urinals where a man as bald as him was urinating. He suddenly went behind the man and kissed his head. The man wasn't pleased, reacted instantly, while looking at 'Charlie':

'I'm not one of them Doreen you know!' Ted at the next urinal responded: 'I *fog* her!'

Charlie couldn't care what he did, continued with emptying his bladder with a smile on his face at the next available urinals. Both Shaun and Edward were watching, ready to protect their patients against any other eventuality. They didn't laugh, but dealt with the situation with understanding. They both knew that they had to accept idiosyncrasies in different individuals, especially when it concerned people with no awareness of their awkward psychological symptoms. They had to guide them and redirect their 'abnormality' away from the so called normally acceptable environment outside.

They returned to the coach with John monitoring entry this time as he stood by the coach door. He had the chance to know Edward better now. He knew about Edward, and what he was up to, but Edward didn't know him. Edward went to sit by him on the coach this time. After a prolonged silence, Edward asked:

'So you are the Activity Organiser, John. You must have just started at Highcroft?'

'Yes, a month ago. But I used to work there before I left for the States,'

'It's obvious by your return that you don't like it there, or may I say you miss your job here?'

'Yes I missed England and the people here, and my girlfriend, whom I am engaged to be married. What about you? You must have just started too?'

'Yes I started in January this year as a student, and am planning to…'

Before Edward had time to finish his sentence, the coach had arrived at Great Yarmouth through big excitement inside the coach. The patients were all ready to get out as the Hotel was only nearby.

'I am getting out first to lead them to the accommodation quarters, while you and your colleagues will follow me, make sure they don't stray,' said John with a smile.

John went to show the downstairs accommodation reserved for patients and staff as instructed, consisted of individual rooms. The nurses' roles were to ensure the patients welfare in their rooms.

As the organiser of the trip, John was the team leader. He had to ensure that the daily leisure activity of the group was maintained. He had to organise daily walks on the beach, playing football, or cricket match with those who could.

But instead of having a wonderful, and an easy time, he was pushy with the patients by forcing them to do things beyond their capabilities. His liaison with the nurses was strained too. On one occasion 'Charlie' ran amok during a game of football. He ran wild and started kissing people around on the head. He was restrained by the staff and brought back to a bench on the beach. John sustained a knock in the event and fainted. Whether the faint was the cause of a genuine knock, or a deliberate act to show his frustration in dealing with the situation, was hard to unravel. Although he wasn't hurt, it definitely revealed a certain weakness in John's general make- up which led to speculation. Thus he maintained a low profile throughout the trip.

Although the incident didn't bother Edward much, he was more concerned about ringing Julie, who had become an obsession now that bugged his mind. He found that he couldn't just stop thinking about her. He looked for a red pay phone box around to ring her, but none to be found. The only one was at the reception of the Hotel. When he went there, he found that there was somebody inside: It was John. He noticed that he was spending a long time inside, ringing Julie perhaps. He went in soon after, saying nothing to John. But disappointingly nobody was at the other end when he rang!

CHAPTER 5

The trip was over the following Saturday, everybody seemed to have enjoyed himself, despite the incidents encountered. Edward was eager to contact Julie on arrival home, but the coach was late. He had to leave it for Monday now. He rang again, Phil answered:

'Oh hello Edward, Julie isn't here. She is at her aunt place. She says she will contact you.'

'OK Mr. Phil, tell her I will see her on Monday,' said Edward.

Monday arrived, Edward was working all day. He spared a few minutes to go to the post office during his break, but the post office was closed. A note on the door was there to say that all business was transferred to the one in Erdington. He speculated then that something was definitely wrong. But Julie rang him on the night, which left a glimmer of hope in him. She didn't want to tell him the truth about their relationship over the phone, in case he became upset and kept ringing her on the night. She only told him the other side of her worry.

'Hi Edward, how was the trip? '

'It was good. How are you anyway? I missed you a lot.'

'Still sad, the Post Office is closed. I don't want to work at the one in Erdington. Sorry I couldn't ring you earlier. I am too upset to talk about it. Can I meet you at Edwards Edwards at 2 p.m. on Wednesday?'

'OK Julie, you sound low in mood, you sure you are all right? I think you should come to my room instead Julie.'

'No I can't. I'm not OK either. I shall tell you all about it on Wednesday.'

'Fine Julie, see you. Love you.'

The conversation terminated with an abrupt end. Edward could sense that everything is not right on the horizon. Julie wasn't herself, because her response sounded too bland. She was acting as though she was talking to a stranger. This was what made him think that apart from losing her job, there was an underlying problem.

The main problem for Julie's was how Edward would take it. She knew that Edward was besotted with her. She loved him too. But she couldn't love two men at the same time, one sexual and one spiritual. Edward seemed to provide all the lovey-dovey romance that John lacked. And John seemed to provide all the sensuality unfulfilled by Edward. In this case scenario she realised that she had to come clean. She knew that hearts would be broken, yet didn't want Edward to suffer the most because of her whims.

John didn't go to see Julie after the trip. He started not to believe in Julie when she told him that Edward hadn't loved her yet. His suspicion became worse when he realised that Edward was a handsome guy, younger than him and that any woman could hardly refuse to get to know him. He thought that the quicker Julie got rid of him, the better it would be for both of them.

But Julie couldn't stop loving Edward that easily, especially as she admired him in many ways. She thought she should have listened to Jane, her working colleague at the post office, who told her once to wait for a while before she embarked on another relationship. But she was too eager to know Edward. Edward was too nice a guy she reckoned to be left alone. Now they both were in a trap, and caught, just because John had returned from America. She wished that John had stayed away. She thought when she went to Edward's room it would be all forgotten the next day if he had bedded her. Unfortunately it didn't happen that way. Edward seemed to have dragged her along in the emotional way, as he refused to transgress the law of love and romance, which was embedded in his faith, despite the fact that he wasn't religious!

John rang Julie soon after Edward did. He seemed to have a lot on his mind. After a long talk about the trip, and 'whom he met' he came to the point:

'You must tell him it's over, and don't see him either. You can't love two blokes as simple as that. I am already planning for our wedding.'

'You know it's not that simple. To be honest with you I have to meet him, John. And I have already arranged to meet him.'

'What! Can I come to clear things up? I know he is a nice guy, I bet he will understand us better.'

'That won't be necessary John. It isn't a matter for us both to get things straight, because I started it.'

'Where are you going to meet him then?'

'Sorry, I can't tell you that. I don't want you to be there either. It won't be in his room anyway, you will have to believe me.'

'I do believe you Julie. And I appreciate your honesty in telling me the truth about him during my absence, instead of going on behind my back.'

'I have learned a lot from him too about faithfulness and sincerity. I'll promise to be honest with you.'

'I trust you then, hoping that he will understand.'

Margaret was listening in the background, and Jill her partner was there too having a glass of wine. Both looked at each other rather surprised, as they couldn't understand why Julie had to go and see Edward again. As soon as John put the phone down, Jill said:

'Surely if she loved you, and you both are planning to get married, she shouldn't go to meet another bloke. Just a phone call will do.'

'That's not the point aunty Jill. She said that she didn't want to offend the guy.'

'Well, well, well that doesn't sound good to me, John,' said Margaret.

'Nor to me mum, but her idea was to tell him the truth about the whole story between her and me,' said John.

'The whole story, do you think he will be interested? He would be more willing to take her away from you! Remember that man isn't one of us, I mean not English. Heather told me he is African. I know those African, and their black magic,' said Jill.

'Are you trying to be funny auntie? There's no way she could go back to him now. You will know why later.'

Both Margaret and Jill looked at each other, perhaps shocked at the anticipation of what would be the good news next to come. But Jill, apart from being nosy, was too anxious to get over the suspense in her usual banter:

'She isn't in the family way is she?' asked Jill.

John gave her an evasive look and went to his bed. He knew that auntie Jill had just 'hit the nail on the head.'

John could hardly sleep on the night. He was thinking like what auntie Jill said: Whether it was proper for Julie to go and see Edward. What would happen if Edward still wanted to take her away from him? Despite of everything Julie could still change her mind about marrying him, and tried to lose her baby! He started blaming himself now for staying away so long without contacting her. He realised that he had to face Edward at work, who surely would know him by now, unless Julie had kept quiet about it. But Julie hadn't met Edward yet! Anyhow he had to prepare to face Edward at some point!

He went to work as usual the next day. During break he saw Edward in the staff dining room having dinner. There were two more female nurses sitting with him by the name June and Jessy. Upon second thought he decided to join them although there were other empty seats around. The dinner looked appetising, they were all enjoying it in profound silence that only their knives and forks could be heard hitting the plates. But by the window somebody with a rather happy face was staring at them while laughing his head off. It was that Smiley again, one of the patients in the *Long Stay Ward*.

'He is a happy soul isn't he?' said Jessy.

'Indeed, he is the only one laughing, and could provide a good distraction for people,' said John.

'He made me laugh too. Remember I am laughing with him as I wave to him!' replied June.

'Look, you are winding him up by waving, June,' said Jessy.

'He is going away now. He had enough by the look of it. I don't know how those 'poor souls' are going to fare as *The Therapeutic Community Program* is underway. They will have to live in the community outside,' Edward butted in the conversation.

'They will be OK Edward, I am involved in this. In living among the 'normal' people outside they will have to learn to reform their ways,' said John.

'You called people outside normal do you?' said Edward smiling.

'What I mean, Edward, is within reasonable conventional standard of society, like propriety,' replied John.

The two girls left the table for the smoke rooms, leaving Edward and John alone. Edward still didn't know about John, as the latter would very much prefer it stayed that way. They would have to enjoy their company for the time being, because the day after tomorrow, Wednesday, circumstances would definitely change. But the fickle minded John, a little nervous, wanted to talk about something else as he didn't know how Edward would respond after his meeting with Julie.

'They are very nice those girls are they, do you know them?' said John, watching the girls leaving.

'We are in the group training together. They are both married, no chance for us! So you are going to find placement in the Community for patients?'

'I surely will, because they are trying to close all the *Long Stay Ward* in the Hospital.'

'Not only in Hospital other business outside too is closing.'

'I know. They closed the Post Office at Stockland Green you know?'

'I know…Oh look at the time. I have to go back… See you again John.'

Edward left, followed by John soon after. Edward didn't mention about Julie at any time during the conversation. John was glad in some way, because he wanted Julie to tell him about her previous relationship. When he mentioned the Post Office, he thought that Edward would tell him a bit more about it, especially about Julie. He was trying hard to get round the fact to know whether Edward was really innocent about his love for Julie!

CHAPTER 6

Wednesday had arrived. Edward wore the same suit he did during his first date to meet Julie at Edwards Edwards in Erdington. He met Julie on the way and gave her a peck on the cheek with a smile. They didn't sit face to face in the coffee shop, but side by side so that he could hold her hand. He ordered two sponge cakes and coffee.

Julie's appearance looked rather downcast. No easy smiles like before, she was more thoughtful. Edward kept looking at her, pretty even when not smiling. He thought her job loss must have impacted her a great deal:

'Never mind Julie you can always try for a job at Highcroft Hospital. All is not lost!'

'It's not about my job Edward it's something else. I don't know how to tell you, because you are too kind to me.'

'Come on, let's have it!'

'I am pregnant!'

'What! Just like that you are pregnant. Goodness gracious, if every woman I kiss, become pregnant, I'll populate the world in no time,' said a shocking Edward.

It's no joke Edward. You know that it couldn't be yours. I come to tell you the truth about John and me, and want to see you too.'

'You have come to see me… If that's the case why you want to see me Julie? You only got to walk away, say nothing. Who is that John anyway?'

Edward asked her, rather bemused, and retiring, suddenly felt like a stranger sitting by her. He released the hand he was holding, and looked at her in the eyes. The shock meant a lot to her, and for him, it was to embark on a journey of despair. All his dreams about the future with her were shattered in an instant. His muse was no more. He had to redraw a pathos now on a new tapestry of time!

He noticed her eyes, her watery eyes. It was the tears of guilt that she inflicted on him. Julie considered him to be the innocent victim. After a short silence she replied:

'John is the man on outing with you from Highcroft. I have known him from childhood, a distant cousin of mine. We started going out nearly a year ago. Then in October he told me to join the Mormons with him which I refused. He said he was going to live with the group. We both called it a day. The next thing I heard he was in America. I said that's it, he will never come back. His mum and I try to contact him. We both wrote so many letters, still no answer from him. Then you came along. I noticed you started admiring me at the Post Office. I felt I had to know you. I seized the opportunity during the Christmas occasion to write you a card. And you preempted the same move to write me one too.'

'Why didn't you let me know you got somebody then Julie? It will save us both from this mess.'

'You never asked me Edward. After all, what's the point? I considered him to be out of my life. I dearly wished he never came back now.'

Julie wiped off a tear from her eye. Edward kept looking at her, while sipping a good mouthful of coffee, leaving the cake alone. Julie didn't touch anything on that table, only the tissue she was holding. Edward didn't know what to say. They both went quiet for a while, only the sound of customers arriving with orders and cutlery could be heard. Appeared subdued as ever, Edward suddenly picked himself up and asked:

'Didn't he call to say he was back?'

'No he just suddenly appeared at home. I saw him the next day. I told him about you, and that we are going to be engaged towards the end of the year. As mum and dad left us alone to visit auntie Maggie, John's mum, you can imagine what happened next.'

'I can imagine what happened all right. So you have come to tell me that you've gone back to John, what I felt for you was just a blow in the wind is it?'

Julie went quiet for a while. She attempted to take a nibble at the cake, but found it hard. She could feel certain shyness developing, difficult to tell whether what she felt then was from her heart.

'It's not like that Edward. I do love you still. I hate John for coming between us. But I want to be true to you in telling you what happened. Now that I am in this predicament, he wanted to marry me in September. But I want to remain friend with you Edward.'

'That's not possible Julie. I don't want to be a threesome. When a single man befriended a married woman, one thing always lead to another...no, no, I don't like that. Better call it a day.'

They both sat down quietly, said nothing. Julie wiped away a tear or two. The middle aged woman serving at the counter was preparing to close the shop for the evening, had been watching them for some time. She had experienced similar scenes in the past. Edwards Edwards had always been the likely platform for dating, or breaking hearts. Without being bashful in their presence, she approached them with some reassuring words:

'Never mind dear, Time is a big healer. You will soon forget about the whole thing.'

'Time and circumstance may change dear, but human emotions don't,' replied Edward, rather disheartened.

Both Julie and Edward looked at each other as they stood up to leave. They walked along the High Street of Erdington not together though, didn't know where they were heading either. They couldn't escape the sight of the towering St Barnabas Church and its tombstones near the road . Edward walked back towards the entrance, not realising that Julie was following. A long bench was by the side, Edward sat there. Julie arrived to sit on the same bench. After a short silence, Julie said:

'Although I know him for so long I don't know if I love him. Since he had forced his way on me, he made sure that I have to love him.'

'What do you expect me to do now, still going out with you? No, I couldn't. Situation might be different if you hadn't slept with him. Now that you have, everything has changed. But remember as time flies, we will be aged, and you will be aged. You will take a good look at yourself then. At 40, 50, or perhaps 60, when the whirl of physical energy is fading, only the spiritual will be left. Loneliness will bug you then into thinking that you should have loved a steadier man instead.'

Edward left her afterwards, and walked back to the nurses' home. Julie left too. Both didn't even look back at each other, but the Church, the house of God stood by, bore witness to their sorrows. Julie went to catch her bus home, feeling dejected as ever. She knew she loved Edward better than John. She considered John to be only part of a loving family which she had grown accustomed to. What she found in Edward was a subtle love, matched by maturity and responsibility.

Edward reached his room feeling bruised and battered. He sat on his bed for a long time, looking at those pictures of Julie on his walls. And at the clock which Julie gave him: The stopping clock still said 4 p.m. He stood up, now he had to get rid of them. He removed all the pictures one by one, leaving only the clock behind. He decided to burn them all the next day.

As far as he was concerned a new chapter would have to start in his life. It had to start now, despite the scars were still there to haunt him. His flatmate, James, living next door to him suspected his anguish as he saw him opening his room door, without saying anything.

He knocked on his door:

'Are you OK mate? Shall we go to the Social for a pint? It's seven p.m.?

Edward opened his door:

'Good idea mate as I'm feeling down in the dump.'

James had started to live in the nurses' home because of his marriage breakup. He was a fully qualified 30 year old nurse, and divorced. As a result of his 'experience' with women, he was ready to have a good talk to Edward. He had seen Edward and Julie a few times, and knew how their relationship had developed. But he wanted to find out more now by Edward's sunken facial appearance.

At the Social Club James went for two pints of Brew XI. He sat by Edward who wasn't used to drinking, but he finished half of his pint in no time, and went to get another one.

'You knocked that back quickly did you? You must be really in trouble!' said James.

'In trouble, not me, it's she!' said a red faced Edward.

'What's happened, did you give her one, and she had a 'bun'…am I right?' James was intrigued.

'Not me mate, it's that sneaky John. I didn't know about him till today.'

'Is it that John, the Social Organiser?'

Edward nodded.

'Cheeky arrogant swine, so he went there first did he?'

'He did indeed I never expected it. He is part of her family, and used to be her boyfriend too. They broke up, but he came back to her house, and they both ended in bed.'

'If she really loves you, she shouldn't have done that.'

'This is what I thought, well too late now.'

'That man deserved a punch in the face. He couldn't be right. He thought he knew all about patients better than us. I heard about him on the Coach trip.'

'I met him on that trip. He knew about me, but never told me about Julie and him, probably out of guilt or shame.'

'Man like him never feel shame mate. You've done well not to continue with her, otherwise it would be too crowded, better leave them alone. Try to catch the right fish now, as there are plenty. I heard he just started to work in the Community, so you won't see him around to give him a mouthful.'

'I won't say anything to him even if I see him. He isn't worth talking to. I've got to get on with my life now.'

'Just like me mate. I don't get involved quickly. You are still young, pass your exam. Travel the world, don't think about women. They will only drive you crazy. When you find a woman, if you start reading Shakespeare loved sonnets or poetry to them, you will only cause more pain. You better get on with it, burn her up! Remember romance and poetry exists only in books and films.'

'You are right mate. I am too much of an artist, and tend to live by a certain principle and motto that's my problem. When she came to my room I should have been there before him. But I hang on, thinking about the morality of the act of consummation before marriage. I have to suffer for it now.'

'You should move with time my friend. We no longer live in the middle age. We do things different now.'

'What's happened with your marriage then, James?'

'Well, you won't understand until you get married Edward. It's a long story, there are always two sides, and the problem in every marriage is different.'

'You got any kids?'

'Boy and a girl, and a lovely house, she got the all lot. I'm an outsider now. But I still see her now and again for the sake of the kids.'

'Any chance of you getting back together, as the saying goes: Absence makes the heart grows fonder.'

'I would say in our case 'no' because she isn't the settled type. After the birth of our second child, we found that there was no love and passion in our marriage. She refused to be tied to a husband and family life. As a result she started to like her freedom to much. She will no doubt think the same about me. Probably she is too young to understand about home life. She may come back to look for me one day.'

'What make you think she will come to look for you? She may find somebody else.'

'I couldn't care if she finds somebody better. She would remember that the first marriage always stays in the memory. The way you fall in love and bring up the first child and so on haunts you… I don't want to talk about it anymore, Edward.'

'Like you say every marriage is an individual thing. Actually this was what I told Julie: One day when she is older, she will come to look for me. I am leaving you to finish your pint now James. I'm too tired, and feel groggy already.'

CHAPTER 7

Edward went to his room to get some sleep, but found it hard to settle. He heard James arrive, accompanied by a female voice in the background. He must have picked up a girl from the club!

Since James had moved to the nurses' home, he had been going out with other girls. His wife, June, knew about it. She couldn't care now anyway, so long as he paid regular maintenance for the family. However they remained good friends, with James paying frequent visits home in Sutton Coldfield, not far from Erdington.

Both June and James were interesting couple, not bad looking either. Although they never neglected their children, they both seemed to have a zest for the outdoor life. June used to have lots of crushes for men. She thought that by marrying James, all her unrealistic infatuations about men would end. But it never did. She remained flirtatious, and in fact she found it harder in the company of men to control her urges. Her latent desires always compelled her to act single again.

Although James said that June wasn't the settled type, he found himself in the worse situation now that he was living on his own in the nurses' home. He became more liberated and forthright with women as if the permissive society currently on going had suddenly released a new lease of life into him. But he found a good friend in Edward, who always had a listening ear to his life story. He thought that Edward was the opposite side of him, being calm, quiet, and reserved. Edward was too much of a prude perhaps who was conscious of the word SHAME.

Sitting on his bed in his room, Edward kept looking at the clock that said 4 p.m., the time that was there when

Julie fixed it to the wall. He couldn't be bothered to even touch it now because it reminded him of his first love, and how he lost it. He still cherished a strong love for Julie though, only if that John hadn't come in between, he thought he would certainly try to settle down to a blissful life. Thinking about James and June, he wondered how people could change their mind in a relationship so easy in England. In Africa people are just as liberated, but are conscious of their responsibilities and duties to their children and community. Once people were married they made sure the marriage last. Although couple fought like cats at times, they hardly get separated.

Edward now lived like a social recluse in his room. He never went to the Social Club despite James attempt to coax him to do so. After work, he continued with his drawings. The previous paintings of Julie on his walls had been disposed of. He found solace in his new paintings, where he could express his emotions. He placed greater importance on beauty, rather than thinking about the seedy side of life. Often the mythological Greek, and Shakespearian tragedies came to his mind, he drew them. The romantic scenery of the Arcadian settings bugged his mind, he drew them. He wanted to make a muse of himself now, using his art as an example of a man in distress to show his romance and passion with a pastoral theme.

Hence he became negligent in his personal care and attitudes. The care and attention he gave to patients at work appeared low in standard, and his daily routine started to affect him. He found himself late a few times for work. His perceptions became somewhat blurred when he looked in the mirror in the morning. A different Edward was there as he didn't bother to shave now. He left his hair all over the place, wore ties that didn't match.

His unkempt appearance raised concern at work. As a butt of all jokes, he was being portrait as a harlequin who entertained patients and staff instead of working as a nurse. Often he was told to prop himself up. He wasn't setting a good example to patients around him.

'Are you OK Edward, you don't seemed to be with it! You are like one of them instead of one of us,' said one of his colleagues with a touch of humour while comparing him with patients of extreme behavioural problems.

Although Edward didn't respond, he was conscious of the fact that he had become too involved with his own problems. His sense of loss was more than palpable. He decided to do something about it. Otherwise it would be detrimental to his mental health. He requested two weeks holidays from the Hospital to visit his home town Soweto, as he had never been back since he arrived in England.

His plan was once on holiday he had to go and visit a 'witch doctor' to get things off his mind. Not that he had no faith in the psychiatrist in England, because if he saw one here, it could tarnish his character. He could indeed be classed 'as one of them', and lost his job. On the other hand he reckoned a psychiatrist dealt with cause and effect, whereas in Soweto they didn't ask questions, the witch doctor there would always know his problems as soon as they saw him.

He got his two weeks holidays, and he arrived in his home village unexpectedly. Because he hardly sent a letter home while in England, everybody thought he was lost. His mum, Pretty, nearly fainted when she saw him at the door: She thought she was dreaming. She noticed the big change in him, with a remarkable weight loss, and a growing a beard that didn't contrast well on his pale skin. But Pretty was happy to see him in person. She was a typical African woman, not bad looking, with dark skin. She lived up to her name as pretty and charismatic.

'Is that you Edward? Let me give you another hug and a kiss to see if you are real,' said Pretty.

'It's me mum, it's me. Sorry got no time to let you know before I came.'

'What have they done to you? You look like you have a big load over your shoulder.'

'I've been working very hard mum. I work as a nurse in mental Hospital now.'

'Good for you son, but be careful about those madman. They can turn you like them if you stay too long with them.'

Edward didn't respond, remained quiet for a while, and looked around him. The pictures he painted of his mum were still hanging on the walls. He saw some village folks were coming to pay him a visit. News of his homecoming had certainly travelled fast. He saw the toddlers he left behind had suddenly shot up, boys and girls he knew had turned into teenagers as if by a magic wand. Within minute his house was full of the locals, and he was in the middle of them.

'How you find England? Do you still draw?' asked Nellie, the next door neighbour.

'England is good, but I have to go back and complete my training at the Hospital.'

'Don't tell me you are going back Edward! Why don't you stay here? There are plenty of jobs in the village now. Auntie Nellie and I will find you a nice girl to marry. Just look at those nice girls around you,' said Pretty.

Edward had already noticed 'those beautiful girls.' They would all certainly make invaluable documents for his drawing. Would he marry one of them, and settle down as his mum said? It seemed that from his bad experience in England, he started to lose trust in women. He wouldn't settle down until he got that load off his mind which kept bothering him now and again. It was the lingering image of Julie of course. This had become an obsession which he thought, had made him lose that confidence. It seemed that time wasn't a healer for him, and he had to see the 'witch doctor' by all means.

In the last week of his holiday, his problem still hadn't gone away it seemed, because he went to the bank and saw a white girl at the counter. And he was in shock when she talked to him! Only his mum was aware about what Edward told her. But in Jabavu the little village where they lived, people had stopped believe in the occult. Christianity had become the popular religion, and western style of living was the norm. He could see the big improvements for himself when he moved around visiting. How big buildings with shopping centres, which weren't there before had transformed small villages into global cities. And looking for a witch doctor in the middle of all these would be a headache. He was sitting at the table with Pretty one morning, and she couldn't believe in what Edward was looking for.

'I take you to see one when you were small Edward because you got worms, now we have real doctors. Are you sure you don't want to see one of them?'

'No, I don't want a medical doctor. He will only give me medicine. I want something for the soul.'

'In this case I have to tell auntie Nellie next door to find you one. She knows more about people in the village than me.'

'Will she keep it a secret, because I don't want people here to know, they will think I am possessed?'

'People are different now Edward. They have changed since you left. What make you have faith in a witch doctor anyway?'

'They don't ask many questions. They treat you as you are. I also want to ask about my father. You never told me about him. You only said that he left you.'

'You don't have to ask anybody about him. Sorry I kept it a secret from you. Since you ask me, I am prepared to tell you, now that I know you are not small anymore. Well, your father and I used to work in the banana plantations. He was a half caste boy, a mulatto, as they used use to call him, a social pariah in those days. I was the only one who accepted him as he was. He got on well with me, and we were both smitten crazy. We started saving up for the wedding, by hiding the money inside the wall where we lived. But one day I arrived home, and found that he left, taking all the money with him. He left me with you in my tummy. Nobody knew where he went. Some said he joined the Army. He must be dead by now as far as I am concerned.'

Pretty became emotional and her eyes started watering. She wiped the tears away with some form of a tissue. Edward felt the pangs of sadness building up in him too, though the situation he experienced was different. He went to sit by her, put his hand on her shoulder, trying to comfort her. They both remained silent for a while, she then continued:

'I was made to feel ashamed as a woman with no husband but with a child inside me. Auntie Nellie next door took me, and looked after me until you were born. You grew up to be a fine boy. You were successful at school, good at drawing too. I deeply appreciated when you helped me out in the fields after school to get more money. But I was concerned that you might do the same with those girls around by making them pregnant and leave them like your father did to me. I used to tell you 'never sleep with a girl until you got married.' I know it's an old fashion thing now, but to maintain happiness after marriage this is essential. It's after marriage that you really find love. I learned from it now after making that mistake, although I never got married.'

'Sorry mum for what you went through. It must have been awful for you when I was still small, and you have to work hard,' said Edward very sad.

'It was hard. But I left you with a good supporting neighbour when I went to work. When you were at home on your own, I bought you some coloured pencils and papers to draw to keep you away from other mischievous children.'

'I knew life was hard this was why I helped out when I left College. I was glad when I was accepted with a visa to go to England. Have you finished paying half of the money I borrowed?'

'I have through sheer hard work, plus some more money you sent. I was glad somehow you went away, because you reminded me of your father with his typical image as you grow up, which I hated. I thought you will never come back since I didn't hear from you. Now that you have, tried to make the best of it, stay here.'

'I have to go back to complete my training. If I stay here you will still hate me like my father,' said Edward smiling.

'But I guess you are different because you came back. Is it because you have that problem in your head?'

'No mum, no, I want to see you too.'

'How that problem affects you so much that you want to see a witch doctor?'

'Because whenever I look at a white girl I saw 'her' there, you know what I mean. Sorry her name gives me the fright. It didn't happen all the time, only when a white girl starts to talk to me. This is what I want to get out of my head, because it affects me at work. It affects me when I go out.'

'But what happens when you talk to a black girl, do you still see 'her'?'

'No, it didn't happen. I went visiting with Sophie. I was OK with her.'

'Sophie is a beautiful girl, and nice too, younger than you. If you like her I can arrange something for you!'

'I have already told her that I love her, that I will come back for her.'

'Love' Edward, that's a very strong word!'

'I know, because we were both smitten.'

'That's very good Edward, are you taking her back with you?'

'No mum, I am thinking of coming back for her.'

'You are coming back when?'

'In two years' time, she said she would wait for me.'

'I am going to see auntie Nellie now to tell her of the good news. I am also going to ask her about the doctor you are on about. I will make sure she keeps it to herself.'

CHAPTER 8

Sophie, auntie Nellie's niece, had just finished her College education. She is dark with the afro hair style that matched her beauty. She had been spending more time at her place alone with her, knowing that Edward was only next door. She had been like Edward's tour guide, visiting places, showing him how their village had improved a lot. Auntie Nellie noticed their innocence at first, but later realised there was more to it, when she saw them holding hands. She thought that they would make a good pair, as she started to observe the open affection they had for each other. She gave more than a good encouragement for their relationship to grow. But at the back of her mind she expected Sophie to remain chaste in her usual reserved manner. She was mindful about any adulterous affair that might develop, where Sophie could end up in the same predicament like Edward's mother, Pretty!

Nellie was having a quiet word with Sophie at the same time that Edward was talking to his mum. She lived on her own since she lost her husband. Her two children lived away with their own families. She was only too glad for Sophie to drop by for a good chat, or gossips perhaps! Sophie seemed to know more about Edward's past history in Soweto than Edward himself realised, because auntie Nellie told her all about it when she knew that the relationship was getting serious.

'Do you think he is going to wait for you until he completes his exams? I suggest that you go with him,' said aunty Nellie.

'He isn't allowed to live with his wife in the Hospital room. He will get a married accommodation when he married me.'

'In that case keep regular contact in writing to him, because remember 'Out of sight, out of mind' as the saying goes?'

'I don't think he will forget me, because he says he is going to paint a picture of me and hang it on his wall, and buy me an engagement ring too.'

'Let's hope he keeps to his word. Remember an engagement ring is nothing these days. At one time it used to be a promise. Did auntie Pretty know about it?'

Pretty appeared soon. After greeted them with a kiss she said:

'Please to know that you and Edward are getting on fine Sophie!'

'I was just going to let you know about the same thing Pretty! It would be good to see them settle down,' said Nellie.

'Edward is on his own at home Sophie, you can go and see him if you like,' said Pretty.

'OK I will. I can take him to the urban areas, as he hadn't been there yet. See you later,' said Sophie.

Sophie left them and went to see Edward.

Pretty sat down in front of a cup of tea Nellie had just made.

'I hope they won't be up to anything, since we both gave them the nod of approval. You can't trust a boy and a girl being left alone in a room these days,' said Pretty.

'Sophie got more sense because I already told her about you raising Edward on your own when his dad disappeared and to try to be respectful and exert some control.'

Both ladies felt a sense of relief when they saw the two lovers walking out of the house soon, holding hands. They were reassured that nothing had happened, but would want to remain hopeful that both Edward and Sophie kept the relationship clean.

'I don't think Edward will do such a thing like his father, however much we resent the saying 'Like father like son,' said Pretty.

'But you can never know do you! So what were you going to say about finding a witch doctor for him? What for Pretty, can't he find a proper doctor in England?'

'He can, but doesn't want people to know about his business. He may lose his job. He is sure that his problem is going to start back once in England.'

'You told me about this white girl he knew and fell for?'

'He only sees her when he talks to other white girls. I don't know how this can happen.'

'Good Lord, this so call civilised world is bringing all sorts of problems for us. At one time such quirky things like that people would just laugh it off easily and done with, now they come back like infected insects to sting people. If he thinks the witch doctor can cure him, so be it. I know one in the Soweto Urban, a long way from here though. We have to catch three buses to get there. We can go in the early morning tomorrow if you like. I know that person is famous to 'kick the devil out of people. Shall we set off in the morning?'

'That will be fine with me. I shall tell Edward then. But keep it a secret Nellie, don't even tell Sophie because she hasn't found anything wrong with him so far. I am sure that doctor will cure him, if he believes in this sort of thing!'

Edward, Nellie and Pretty left the next morning in the hot sun. They took their bus as mentioned to get to the Soweto Urban. The first bus travelled on a tar road which was smooth. The next one travelled on cobbles and pebbles, a bit rough, and the third one travelled on dusty bare brown grounds, enough to make passenger felt the bumps amidst the flying dust. It was this bus that would drive them into a different world.

Travellers in that bus, through their own idiosyncrasies, could reveal that they too were victims of some disordered state of the mind. They were all on their way to seek a stable life. They laughed out loud for no apparent reasons while sitting on their own. Some grimaced by gesturing to one another. And some talked out loud to nobody. Amidst this sort of bedlam which Edward wasn't new of course, he was unconcerned as he was one of those misfits!

Edward watched the bus meandering through the narrow lanes in the woodlands, hitting watery pot holes and went over tree carcasses. Bushy trees and thick hedgerows on both sides of the roads also complimented the journey, along with the strong smell of dung. The bus reached its destination at last. It came to a standstill in the middle of nowhere. Drumbeats could be heard with people shouting.

On the plane field some shanty houses could be seen with thatched roofs about to drop. But some did drop as they were on the ground instead, leaving the bare walls to stand on their own. Scantily clad folks still seemed to use the roofs, as they had made doors in them! Undernourished looking cattle were moving freely, and there were cows' drawn carts with heavy load of hay plodding the muddy tracks in the fields. The whole environment depicted a dystopian scene that hadn't changed with time.

After a short while a half- naked man that look like a guide, with only long leaves covering his private parts approached the bus. The driver exchanged a few words noisily with him. They were talking the old African lingo that neither Nellie nor Pretty could understand. The driver told all the passengers to follow the guide, but Edward jumped the queue, and gestured to both his mum and auntie Nellie to do what he did as he was anxious to be treated first, and done with.

They were all led through a narrow bushy path in the direction of the drumbeats. The beats became sharper as they approached an open ground. Three natives dressed just like the guide, had their drums hanging from their necks down were all dancing with the rhythm. In the midst of them a fire eater performed his various tricks, interspersed by hitting the air with a broomstick of some sort. The whole choreographic display was supposed to ward off evil spirits around the area.

Somebody came out of a straw roof hut dressed like the others but with a white painted face and large ear rings, wearing a green leafy hat. He was Banu, the witch doctor, enough to make Edward think that he was having nightmares already. He asked Edward to follow him, leaving Nellie and Pretty behind.

Once inside the hut, they both sat opposite each other on the floor by a fire that kept burning continuously. There were also some artefacts, like black and white small barnacle shells in a jar. Burning josticks pricking onto bananas bombarded the air around with a magic aroma of incense.

Banu glanced at Edward with his piercing glittering eye that went through him. He asked him in English:

'You from England, have woman's problem?'

'How do you know that, Sir?'

'Banu knows everything about people who came to see me. There is somebody here who tells me.'

Edward looked around, didn't see anybody.

Banu continued:

'Look at me now there is something in your head which I want to get rid of.'

Edward appeared sleepy, and sweaty likely to drop off. Banu took the jar containing the shells. He opened it and flung the content on the floor by Edward. He asked Edward to pick one of the shells. He picked one of the white ones and gave it to Banu.

The witch doctor had a good look at it, grimacing with a sardonic smile, and said something which only he could understand. He then threw it in the burning fire that exploded with a pop.

'It's that white woman. You must leave her alone. Another woman is in your life now. You will marry her! You will have two children.'

Banu then stood up, leaving Edward sitting in a trance like state. He stood in front of him, placed his right hand palm on his forehead, mumbled something again and pushed his head forcibly backward a few times. This was enough to wake Edward up from the trance as he could hear the drumbeats louder.

'I have finished with you now. You can go. When any thoughts tried to mislead you just say 'Banu.' This will drive it away.'

Edward said nothing still dazed. On his way out he fumbled in his pocket, took whatever changes that came into his grasp, gave them as donations. He noticed that the group he arrived with had dwindled. The drummers had disappeared too. It seemed there were many Banus at work in this area, doing their own thing in their huts.

Outside, both Nellie and Pretty met up with him as he was still in a dream. They went on both sides of him to lead him through the narrow path into the same bus that brought them here. They were the last one to get in before the bus left. Inside the passengers were all sparked out like they had been coshed, a big difference from the rowdy scene experienced before! Even Edward fell fast asleep.

'The driver would have a big job to wake them up when we reached the next stop,' said Pretty.

'Probably he is used to it. They all seemed to have been cured by the look of it!' replied Nellie.

'I hope so. Edward will be glad it's over,' said Pretty.

The bus slowed down after a while. The driver boomed:

'We've reached the first stop, anybody getting out?'

Nobody budged. He walked along the seats of passengers to wake them up. There were some responses then. A few of them suddenly open their eyes. They looked as normal as they could possibly be. They got down from the bus without any fuss. Pretty gave Nellie a surprise look and said:

'What a big difference Nellie. It had worked for them. Let's hope Edward would feel the change too.'

CHAPTER 9

Before the last bus stopped in Edward's home town, he was fully awake. Still he didn't know whether the nightmare in his head had gone. He would have to come across a white girl, but it would be hard to see one in the area, only at the bank perhaps.

'How do you feel now Edward? We are nearly home. I bet Sophie will be waiting for you,' said Nellie.

'Did you tell her where we were going auntie?' asked Edward.

'No I didn't, but being so intuitive, she would have some premonition of some sort that we went to the 'Fairy Land' as they call it, if she knows we took three buses, and arrived back at dusk.'

Edward went quiet for a while. He was trying to develop a more positive attitude about the whole thing. Even if Sophie knew, would she be put off by him going out there where only the so called 'nutters' go for a desperate cure? But he found Sophie very understanding since the short time he had known her. He was sure she would support him. He had to be honest and came out with the truth about his problems in order to build a trusting relationship. He decided to tell Sophie himself.

Sophie's dad Paul, Nellie's brother in law, and his wife, Tessa were very keen for Sophie to marry Edward, as they too noticed how the love between them had blossomed. They both cherished the idea of Sophie to lead a progressive life abroad, because there wasn't much prospect in Soweto for a girl. They liked Edward, not because he was handsome, but his placid nature and profession, entrusted them with the confidence that he was an ideal man for their daughter. They were sure that

Edward would pop the question for their daughter's hand before he left for England.

Pretty and Edward invited Nellie for some tea when they arrived at home. Sophie arrived soon after, eager to join them for a chat as she saw Edward arrived exhausted from the journey. But she didn't beat about the bush. With her usual banter, she was intrigued by the journey they made, when she knew that they took three buses to get there.

'You didn't go to the 'Fairy Land' did you?' she asked.

Despite the exhaustion of their journey, and trying to keep cool under the ceiling fan, they all got a smile on their faces. But only Edward replied:

'Yes we did Sophie, a Fairy Land indeed. I am still half asleep.'

'It was exciting to see something different. Edward wanted to know about his future! Shall we go to my place next door Pretty to prepare a meal. You two can come later as I have invited both Paul and Tessa to come along too since you are leaving us the day after tomorrow Edward,' said Nellie.

'Good idea auntie Nellie. I wish I could take her with me, but we both have to be married first to get the right papers for the immigration, it's a bit too late now,' said Edward.

'Good lad, see you next door soon,' said Nellie.

Nellie and Pretty went next door to prepare the meal. It was no big deal for them as they both enjoyed cooking.

Sophie and Edward moved closer to each other when being left on their own. They both stood up, started hugging and kissing each other, while the ceiling fan went spinning round and round to cool them down. They sat down very close to each other again:

'What did you ask the doctor then Edward?'

'I didn't ask for anything. He is well known to tell people's problems before they open their mouth. He said we are going to get married and have two children.'

'Is that so, what would happen if I change my mind about marrying you?'

'I hope you don't Sophie because I love you a lot. I shall miss you very much when I am in England. As you are aware that I intend to draw your picture, can you come to town with me tomorrow to get some drawing materials?'

'I shall certainly do that Edward, but you haven't finished yet in telling me what that doctor did and said to you. Why did you go to see him in the first place?'

'Please Sophie don't think bad of me if I tell you that another girl I finished with, kept coming back to my head when I talk to any white girl. I went to the doctor, and he knew my problem. He said he had cured me after driving me in a trance using the various manipulations around him.'

'What did you do to the white girl then for her to haunt you?'

'I only drew her picture and kiss her.'

'Do you still see her in your head when you kiss me? What else did you do to her?'

'I swear to God nothing else. You have to trust me Sophie. It only occurs whenever I talk to a white girl.'

Sophie's appearance suddenly changed from being cheerful to a more thoughtful and worried looking girl. She became silent for a while, thinking how the future would fare for them, if Edward still had that 'thing' in his head, but remained hopeful that Edward was cured.

Sitting by her, hand in hand, absorbed in the serenity that dwelled on her facial countenance, he constantly admired her good looks. He gave her a hug and a kiss in between. With Edward's reassurance Sophie continued to be supportive. She hadn't seen anything wrong with Edward so far. She desperately wanted to experience for herself how Edward would feel when he talked to white girls. She knew the only place she could find some were behind the bank counters. There would be an opportunity to watch Edward on the next day when they went to town she thought.

'I can give you my word in not telling my parents about your problem Edward.'

'OK I trust you Sophie… Hang on I heard somebody coming.'

Paul appeared at the door:

'Come on you young lovers, you are wanted next door,' said Paul.

'Oh dad, we are coming,' replied Sophie.

They all went next door amidst the aroma of a splendid meal of some sort. A big enough table was laid out to accommodate everybody. Edward kept looking at Sophie who sat beside her. He was already besotted by her charm. He wished he had stayed longer now, he never thought he would find the love of his life during his short spell in Soweto, considering he only came back 'because of that thing' in his head. The verdict still had to come out tomorrow at the bank!

Everybody seemed to enjoy the delicious meal, and praised Nellie for her culinary skills. They wondered if Edward enjoyed such delicacies in England.

'How is the English food then Edward? Do you like it?' asked Paul.

'Do you cook your food yourself?' asked Tessa.

'No auntie Tessa I received free cooked food from the canteen, but the food is not as nice as the ones here, especially when it's being cooked by auntie Nellie,' said Edward, turning to Nellie with a smile.

'I am honoured of so much praise for my cooking, remember Pretty helped me out too. Thanks everybody, glad that you all enjoyed it. But tell us about the fish and chips and boiled meat in England Edward. I heard they don't use spice at all there,' asked Nellie.

'We have spicy food in England auntie Nellie in Indian restaurant. But in other restaurant, and Hospital canteen, they haven't grown to like the rich spice yet, so most of the meat is boiled. I have to eat them, otherwise I'll be starving. As for the fish and chips on street corners, they are good for a quick bite when somebody is peckish.'

Everybody went quiet at the table. Pretty then changed the tone of the conversation, and embarked on something different. She had to make a move about what everybody was observing while sitting at the table: Edward's dreamy eyes and the sympathetic look he cast on Sophie's face was enough to signify the love bond he formed that had to be loosen soon.

'Just to let you know Paul, Edward found his love rather late. He couldn't get married at such a short notice. I am sure he will come back for her, unless Sophie decided to go there to marry him, because she is planning to do nursing too,' said Pretty.

'Is that so, how come you never told us Sophie?' asked Tessa.

'I want to give all of you a surprise, mum,' replied Sophie.

'A surprise indeed, where are you planning to be trained Sophie?' asked Edward.

'Obviously at your place to keep an eye on you Edward, my application had been forwarded already!' replied Sophie.

'Good news indeed, you are a fast mover are you? How did you get my address Sophie?'

'I thought I told auntie Pretty to keep it a secret when I asked her for your Hospital address, but somehow she lets it out. Now that you know about it, you can put a good word for me when you reached there.'

'Sure I will Sophie, very glad indeed.'

Edward noticed how animated Sophie had become. Sophie was confident that she would be accepted. Even if not at the same Hospital, she would certainly get somewhere else nearby as she had the right qualifications. But she had another surprise up her sleeve: She waved her left hand with a ring on a finger in the air in a jubilant mood and said:

'Look I am engaged too!'

'Now, that is a big surprise!' said an enthused Paul.

Nobody expected this after dinner. It was something to be remembered. Edward brought that ring from England, intended for Julie, and was hopeful that, should he find somebody, he would be glad to give it away. He was glad he found that person, and fortunate too that the ring fitted nicely on Sophie's finger.

Everybody relished the wonderful occasion now that the good news had filled them with a renewed excitement.

They all hugged the pair with congratulatory kisses, and good wishes.

Pretty hugged Paul, Tessa and Nellie, welcomed them into his family, although the wedding wasn't yet fixed. Nellie's house was transformed into more than a party atmosphere that night, as the two families were on the way to merge into one.

CHAPTER 10

The next day Sophie and Edward went to town to buy the drawing materials as planned. Edward decided to use various shades of black for the drawing by applying paint along with wax crayons on a thick white background of blank paper. He also got the correct sized paper that wouldn't be damaged on his way back to England.

They both appeared more confident now, knowing that fate had brought them together. Edward was sure that he would self-fulfil that prophesy the witch doctor told him. Not because he devotedly believed in the weird things he did, but because he started to regain a certain free will that went out of control. He felt like a new man now that had been purged of his past sorrows, and ready to settle down with Sophie whatever it took. Still at the back of his mind he had to leave for England on the next day. It would be hard for him to stomach this. It would be like leaving part of him behind. He was glad that Sophie would try her best to join him in England. The quicker the better he thought.

In town Sophie came across a hair dressing saloon. Holding Edward's hand tightly she glanced over sample of excellent hair styles displayed through the window. They both looked at each other smiling, but Edward anticipated the one she liked most that would suit her, and made easy drawing too. He gave her a treat for the chosen one, and sat down waiting while the hair dresser was at work.

He observed how her loosed curly black hair was straightened to near shoulder length after being washed and heated. How the transformation gave a new theme to her appearance that highlighted her beauty. Edward was pleased at what he saw, and Sophie was pleased with her new look.

'You look stunning Sophie. A shame I have to leave you tomorrow, shall we take a picture together at the photo studio? I know we won't get it till after I left, but you can always send a copy to me by post.'

Edward proceeded to give her a hug and a kiss on the way out.

'OK Edward thanks for liking my new look. I would like to have our picture taken.'

After leaving the studio, they both went to the bank. There were two white girls working at the counter. They both seemed to look alike, despite the difference in hair styles and colour. Edward looked at Sophie with a smile, and Sophie smiled back. He didn't show any form of anxiety. He was reassured with Sophie in front of him in the queue, and by the fact what to do in case he saw 'something different' when the girls started to talk to him.

When Edward's turn arrived, one of the girls serving him became very chatty. She wanted to know which part of Birmingham he was from:

'I am from Birmingham too, but know Erdington very well,' she said.

'So you live here permanently now?' asked Edward.

'I am here on contract for two years before I go back to England,' she replied.

'I'm going back tomorrow,' said Edward.

Sophie's desperation to find out the outcome after this conversation, nudged Edward to come out with her. Edward seemed relaxed, was glad that he didn't have to say 'Banu' after all, like what his 'doctor' told him to do.

On the way home, the two lovers walked hand in hand.

'I am over the moon Sophie, and very pleased, that 'thing' is no more. I don't think it will ever come back because I felt I am myself again. I could feel it Sophie, I could feel it.'

'What can you feel Edward?'

'I can feel my head clearer, that's good news. At first I was a little apprehensive when I talked, with the two of them in front of me, but nothing happen while I was listening to them.'

'You shouldn't enjoy chatting to the girls now as they may lead you astray again!' said Sophie with an easy bantering that raised concern for Edward. But he heeded at what Sophie said, and didn't want to make Sophie jealous. He reassured her:

'You shouldn't worry about that Sophie, although in my profession I am surrounded by them, or me surrounding them! You can't say that all girls in England are easy going with men, ready to jump into bed with them, all girls aren't the same. I also respect girls for what they are. But men do get carried away sometimes that's their weakest point.'

'You can say that again Edward because men carry a stronger urge. Some women do too, but they seem to be more in control because they possess more dignity and respect. Only those who think less of themselves do stray as their personal worth has no significance for them. I am glad you have got over your problem now. But while in different part of the world, we both have to be sincere and faithful to each other. I am a bit old fashion like auntie Nellie. She told me a lot about how men behaved, but of course not all men are the same like you said. I find that you are a more understanding person, this is why auntie

Nellie likes you, and I fall for you. You have never tried to act your instinct out on me which I like most despite that we are engaged to be married. I appreciate too that you welcome the fact of me coming to join you in England. I wish I am accepted in the same Hospital where you work.'

'I'm sure you'll be accepted because they are short of staff there. Again I shall put a kind word for you with my boss. I can't wait to see you with me. We shall get married as soon as you get there in the registry then celebrated it in grand style when we return on holidays.'

But Sophie was more concerned about the girl Edward finished with, whether she still worked near his place.

'Do you still see that 'girl' near your work place? Is she married now?'

'No Julie doesn't work at the post office anymore, she left the area altogether, she may be married by now. Let's change subject shall we? I don't want to talk about her. Let's go home I desperately want to draw that picture of yours.'

Edward had certainly been cured of his problem by the ease he mentioned Julie's name without any reluctance. Previously that name would spell anxiety for him. Although he didn't tell Sophie the whole story, he tried to be cautious in not letting everything out. He knew Sophie was a decent girl, and the price of jealousy was too dear a legacy to be left behind.

They arrived home, had a quick meal, he put his crayons into action straight away. He asked Sophie to sit on a stool in front of him, while Nellie, who liked Sophie's new look, went next door, and left them alone.

He admired Sophie's whole profile and beauty after Sophie applied extra makeup on. Edward thought that her new look suited her very well. She became an instant muse to inspire him with the emotional energy that would make a visual feast to his senses. For him it would be a brush stroke applied with care dedicated only to the chosen one that would grace the wall of his room.

He drew the contour of her whole face first. He then applied a thin layer of black background around it, while leaving the inside of the face with a different shade. He measured the distance and the facial expression, with some good humour to go with to make her laugh, so that he could observe her all being.

'Remember I'm not a street artist nor am I contemplating of drawing something grand like Van Gogh, but something worth to remember you by.'

'Oh Edward you are funny,' said a smiling Sophie.

She continued:

'Don't draw me like a graffiti artist, will you?' said Sophie teasing him with a smile.

'The best graffiti can be a work art my dear,' replied Edward with a smile, carry on drawing.

'You are right..!'

Sophie appeared to be moving too much. Edward could sense the impatience and fidgety in Sophie as he was taking too much time.

'Hang on, hang on stay there. I have to get that nose and those lovely eyes right.'

After placing the finishing touch to the drawing, Edward showed it to Sophie.

'That's an excellent piece of art Edward, it's a shame you can't do me a self- portrait of you!'

I am afraid you'll have to do this one Sophie. Never mind, when you come over to England I'll show you how to draw one. I'm sure you'll make a very good one.'

'What make you say that Edward?'

'Well, you've got that pause, and a good composure matched by an ability to concentrate.'

'We shall see Edward! Shall we ask auntie Nellie to cook something I'm starving?'

Nellie and Pretty arrived just on time.

'How do you like this,' Edward showing the drawing to them.

'Very good Edward just like a drawing from a professional,' said Nellie.

'I told you how good he was Nellie! And Sophie's new hair style, do make a lot of difference. I like that very much!' said Pretty.

'Why don't you do this for people I bet it will fetch you some money!' said Nellie.

'I shall think about this one. It will be another career for me, said Edward.'

'Shall we go and have something to eat?' said Nellie.

'Good idea, then, Edward will have to get prepared after, for his departure tomorrow at noon. I bet it will be a sad day for him,' said Pretty.

'I hate to leave you all tomorrow. I know it will be hard for me on that day. I never expected such a welcoming gesture from everybody here, and I thank auntie Nellie to introduce me to the love of my life. I remember when

I left Jabavu, Sophie was small. I am amazed how she has grown so quickly. I will dearly miss her, and everybody of course,' said Edward.

'I think Paul and Tessa want to see all of us tonight at his place for dinner, since you are leaving for the airport early morning,' said Nellie.

'OK we shall attend, but I shall have to come back early to arrange my suitcase,' said Edward.

CHAPTER 11

Paul and Tessa welcomed their guest on the night. They all sat down at the table to have their meals. Edward and Sophie started to feel the pangs of departure and separation already. They could feel the bond binding them together would be loosened soon. Closed by each other they sat, holding hands, with intermittent smiles, saying less. Paul had brought some wine this time to celebrate the occasion and to cheer the couple up. He wanted to find out if Edward was true to his word in his proposition of marriage to Sophie, not a flight of fancy. He knew about certain men when they came on holidays, they started flirting with the girls then never heard from them again, once they were abroad.

'When are you coming back to see us again Edward? I hope you won't leave it long, because we are all eager to see you two, tie the knot soon,' said Paul.

'If he doesn't come back, I'll be there anyway to make him do. Hoping I am going to be accepted for training at his Hospital,' said Sophie smiling.

'I'm sure you will Sophie, looking forward to see you there,' said Edward.

Edward felt more confident when he spoke, which gave the family the reassurance that he meant what he said, especially as Sophie would surely join him, perhaps got married in England.

Nellie had been observing Edward since he arrived. She seemed to know a decent man when she saw one, but she still had her reservations. It was she who had been given Sophie some good advice when she saw romance in the air. How they had spent almost every day in each other's company during the short spell he was there. Although they were physically attracted to each other, she sincerely wanted the relationship to be kept innocent and pure. She was no prude but she expected some behavioural standard in her family, and wanted Sophie to retain that sense of self-worth, not to express her individuality in excess despite the liberal attitudes of the time.

In the small community where she and Pretty lived, it was like a big family. Each one seemed to know about the other, so the question of honour could become the talk of the village. Edward too was aware about honour and legacy. He deeply regretted his own mum's plight before he was born when she had to run the gauntlet of discontentment living as a single pregnant woman in the community.

Pretty and Edward left Sophie's family after dinner to get the suitcase ready for the early morning departure. They would all accompany him in a taxi to the airport which had been ordered by Paul.

Everybody was obviously sad to see Edward leaving at the airport. Pretty wiped off a tear or two, Sophie became speechless as if mesmerized, seeing the plane revving mad on the tarmac. Nellie was busy comforting her with her gentle smiles. When Edward finished sorting out all his papers, he gave everybody a hug, but gave Sophie more than a hug before he left to board!

The plane took off amidst the waving crowd of friends and relatives at the airport, while Edward found himself alone again among the passengers on board. But he felt relief by the fact that his problem hadn't started anew with all the girls he came across. He had been cured, and he was glad!

The plane touched down at Birmingham Airport late. He took a taxi to get back home.

On arrival, his flat mate James saw him coming in the corridor. He was thrilled to see Edward as he open his room door.

'Hello Edward how did it go then? Had a nice time did you?' James went to shake his hand like welcoming him back, and accompanied him in his room for a chat. They both sat down, as Edward dragged his suitcase on the floor in his room.

'Yes mate, I wished I could stay longer if I don't have to get back to work in the morning.'

'You know you look great, like a different bloke, since I last saw you. The holiday must have done something good to you. Please tell me where you went, I wish I can go there myself as I felt really down at the moment!' said James yawning.

'Why, what did you do James?'

'Nothing, it's that wife of mine. She is playing me up. She asked me to take the kids away for a while. When I get back she was with somebody else.'

'You are both divorced aren't you, why you worry about her then?'

'It isn't nice to see that sort of thing even when you are divorced Edward. It really hits me. I don't want to talk about it. Anyway it's past midnight. I better leave you as you are on the early. We shall chat another time. By the way I am going on a nursing course myself tomorrow morning in Manchester. I shall see you when I get back in a week time.'

'I shall see you then James, good night. I'm tired too. I think I go to bed straightaway.'

James and Edward were the only two staff that lived upstairs. There were a few living downstairs, but Edward was more used to his friend James. He was hoping that on his way back he would be in his good company to cheer him up as he would definitely feel the jet-lag and loneliness, after he had been surrounded by his loved ones in Soweto. Now he would have to go for a drink on his own, or spending his time drawing in his room.

He went to work the next day, and everybody saw the big change in his general appearance as he had no beard. He was pleased that he could work with a clear, fresh head now, without having to endure the butt of all jokes like before. Although a little tanned, his good looking feature could still make him a popular figure. He had to work a long day. After work he arrived back to sort out his suitcase, and to arrange the things he brought with him. The first thing he took out was Sophie's picture that he drew. He was glad that it was left intact despite the strain of the long journey travelling. He thought that Sophie did a good job there in wrapping it in an excellent package. He kept looking at it, and where should it go on the wall of his room. He finally decided to place it where one of Julie's favourite pictures was: by his bed!

The next day he was off all day. He went to the High Street in Erdington to buy a few things he needed for his drawings. He wanted to make a more refined picture of Sophie, on canvas this time and in colour!

The Art Shop by the post office was well known for selling various artefacts for painters. This was where some staff from the Art Therapy Department of Highcroft Hospital went to buy art materials to engage patients in art: The Therapy Unit also formed part of the social organising to help patients out in expressing themselves through their paintings, which psychologist could use to interpret their emotions.

In the shop Edward was going through all the canvas, looking for the appropriate size for the wall of his room. He found himself standing by somebody whom he wished he had never met: It was John, the future husband of Julie. He too was buying a few drawing artefacts but for the Therapy Department of the Hospital. John didn't realise he was standing by Edward. As soon as he turned his head, he was shocked to find Edward without a beard now, and looking more of himself.

'Hello Edward, I never knew you are a painter,' said John holding his hand out for Edward to shake. However disappointed Edward was by having to come across him again, as a gesture of goodwill, he shook his hand in a lukewarm fashion, and in a manner that said it all: disgusting!

'Hi.. I always like to draw,' replied Edward rather reluctant to talk.

'You look well mate. I heard you went on holiday.'

'Yes I did,' replied Edward, uninterested to talk any further. But John wanted to lessen the bitterness between them by recuperating a last move as he said:

'Sorry Edward I took Julie from you. I wish it didn't happen that way, no hard feelings.'

He held out his hand to shake again, but Edward just gave him such repulsive look that he walked away, buying nothing.

In his flat Edward spent no time to get started with his drawing of Sophie again. He could place the brief unfriendly encounter at the Art shop at the back of his mind easily now. He already had a table and a chair which he conveniently positioned to do all his drawings.

He was working early on the next day. He carried on with the drawing in the afternoon after work. Nobody was upstairs to distract him, and the lingering silence in the evening was ideal for him he thought. He planned to give a real masterpiece to the art world. He kept musing at the picture of Sophie on the wall, and placed what he could perceive on canvas. Her inspiring figure, gave him enough vibrancy to drive him into a utopian world, where only the good and the kind lived. But his dreams were shattered when he heard audible footsteps creeping in the corridor upstairs and stopped by his door. He was intrigued, he opened his door. What he saw he couldn't believe. He thought he wasn't on planet earth: It was a pretty, ginger haired, voluptuous young woman, wearing hot pants and a light top, fashionable at the time. And her strong perfumed seemed to bombard the corridor.

'Oh.hello you are Edward are you?' she asked smiling.

'Yes I am do I know you?' replied Edward, trying to avoid her gaze, but didn't know where to look either!

'I am June, James ex-wife, have you seen him?'

'I am afraid he is away on a course.'

'Sorry I don't know.'

Edward couldn't take his eyes off her afterwards, but since she was his friend's ex-wife, he invited her for a cup of tea.

June gladly accepted the invitation, came inside and made herself at home, sat on his bed. Edward noticed that she wasn't sober.

'You are a good painter are you? I heard all about you,' said June.

'Who have been talking about me then?'

'James told me about your drawings, how good you are. Who is that you are drawing now?'

'She is my girlfriend whom I met during my holiday.'

'Is it the same like the one hanging there? She is pretty isn't she, and decent looking too, not liked me, enjoying the good life.'

Edward, looked thoughtful, placed a few touches to his drawing in front of him. He continued:

'Can you tell me more about your good life June?'

'Good life, oh Edward, it means kick out your husband, getting sloshed when you want, and be free. Where is that drink you promise me then?' June replied smiling, with a slight banter, as she moved closer to Edward's chair. The heavy smell of alcohol started to become more pronounced than her perfume, but Edward unimpressed, stood up to make the drink as the kettle was already boiled. He made her a strong cup of coffee instead to sober her up. He gave her the cup which she took a sip before resting it on a table nearby. She looked at the picture on the wall again and said:

'Can you draw me like the one on your wall Edward?'

June removed her flimsy top off, leaving only her black bra suspending her breasts.

She smiled and continued:

'I can bare all you know!'

'That won't be necessary June. It's revealing as it is. I can do a quick outline of your face, down to your neck, not on canvas though!'

Edward placed Sophie's drawing aside, took a blank sheet of paper, and started to draw her face. June became edgy, could hardly keep still. Edward noticed she was tired, as her eyes were closing on and off.

'Don't you think you'll be better at home on your bed June?'

'No, I want to sleep here like that Edward,' said June, lying backward, and spreading herself.

Edward reacted with shock suddenly, and replied:

'You can't June. If you sleep here I will be in trouble, because the security guards normally visit after midnight. If they hear somebody in my room, they would like to know who. I could be expelled from the home if they found you, and I have to live outside renting then.'

June sat on the bed again while rubbing her eyes yawning:

'OK love, I am going then since you don't want me,' she said as she stood up, 'Can you give me that unfinished picture then?'

Edward couldn't wait to give her the half drawn picture to get rid of her. She took it and had a look:

'It's coming up nicely, a shame I have to leave. I can come back for you to finish it you know.'

'I don't think I'll be interested June. James will be here tomorrow.'

'Never mind him. I do what I want. He is no good.'

June put her top on. She forgot the picture on the bed, and Edward opened the door for her. Half way out she held Edward and gave him a big kiss before she left.

Edward couldn't wait to see the back of her. It was the biggest titillation he ever had to cope with. He didn't have to say 'Banu' as stated by the witch doctor in Soweto. During the struggle in his mind, whether to succumb to his desire or defy the 'temptation,' he had the image of Sophie etched on his mind now. He had to remain pure and faithful, not tarnish the promise he made to her. He got no wish to fuel the sparks, and causing the flame to spread during the encounter, as he was aware of that animal instinct. In trying hard not to let it come out to the fore, he was very much in control. After all, he didn't want to take advantage of the weakness in human nature to grab the easy prey to satisfy him!

He carried on with his drawing not letting the distraction drove him off course. It had become like a routine for him, whenever he was off, his painting took the centre stage.

Saturday had arrived and James was back. James would definitely know if his wife had been to see him, because although divorced, June liked to show him off in front of other people to get the attention she craved. She was like a stage character who liked to dramatize events in her life at the expense of her husband. But James had enough of her, desperately wanted her to get out of his life.

CHAPTER 12

Edward went to see James in his room. Not to show his innocence about June's recent visit, but to have a general chat about how he got on. James had thoroughly enjoyed the course on Mental Health, but seemed rather sullen with other private matters bothering him. He knew that his wife had been at his flat looking for him because he never had a chance to tell her of his absence. Apparently he went to the house at the last minute before he left for Manchester, nobody were there. He went again on the way back, and he had an awful argument with June, who accused him of domestic violence which he said was untrue.

'I can't see you using violence James. You are too understanding and placid. She came here you know, looking for you. She was tipsy,' said Edward.

'I know she did. You should have given her one!'

'Surely you don't mean it that way James. I wouldn't do that in the state she was, however much the titillation.'

'You are a good man Edward. Sorry for what I said. I am going to live in Manchester you know, I manage to find a job in another Hospital there. How about you? How was your holiday then?'

'I got on well, managed to find what I wanted. I also fell for somebody. She is coming here to do nursing too.'

'Excellent Edward, you look better for it too, glad you got over that problem in your head. What did you do?'

'Well, I went there for something different, away from the conventional treatment in England, and that, challenged my perceptions on mental health. It may not work for everybody though!'

You must tell me something more about that sometimes, I could do with some of that.'

James went to Edward's room afterwards, eager to see how Sophie looked like, and he was given a few things Edward brought from Africa.

'A very attractive girl you've got there Edward. I'm glad for you. You are drawing her again are you? It is certainly looking good,' said James, after having a look at the drawing.

'When are you leaving then?' asked Edward.

'Fairly soon, but don't tell anybody about it till the day I'll leave.'

'You can trust me James. I may come out of here too when Sophie arrives. We shall have to rent a room outside, live in sin till we got married.'

'Good idea mate. I think you better get a room outside before she arrives. She can come straight to you then.'

'I think I will James.'

James left Highcroft Hospital two weeks later. Edward found himself on his own upstairs again. He had completed his excellent piece of work of Sophie which he hanged on his wall. Being on his own, he didn't want to be disturbed by June's presence once more, especially as she forgot to take the unfinished picture of her when she left the last time. No way could Edward go back to that picture now as it gave him the creeps. Hence he destroyed it. He decided to move out to a rented accommodation on Slade Road nearby, big enough to accommodate two people.

In Soweto, Sophie was delighted to have been accepted as a student nurse at Highcroft Hospital. And Edward was over the moon too. Aunty Nellie and her mum Pretty were happy for her to meet Edward in England. They had both told her to get married sooner as planned, no matter whether they wished to come back to Soweto or not. To dispel their suspicions, and fears, Edward reassured them in ringing them despite the cost of phone calls. He promised to send the registry wedding pictures to them.

A month after Sophie set foot in England, they got married. They both completed their exams in psychiatric nursing after three years, and moved to a house which they bought near Erdington village. They visited Soweto afterwards. They had their first child, a boy Jim and a girl Tessa, in the following years.

But like all marriages, although they were happy, it wasn't without any humps and bumps. Edward seemed to be carried away too much with his drawings. It was the only way he could be in touch with how his mind looked at the world 'through the window of his soul.' But he never wanted to part with any of his paintings, which he reckoned were too precious and regretful for him to give away. His walls at home were like a gallery. Sophie was left with a handful of domestic duties as a result, like having to look after the children, doing house works, cooking and be a nurse. She had observed Edward's neglect in the house, which Edward refuted as untrue, a female misconception of a male dominance perhaps which was an instinctive perception in any marital relationship, that a male is the stronger sex, had to leave the wife doing all the house works!

Sophie being calm, with a relaxed appearance as usual, kept her house unlike any traditional reserved African woman. She showed her individuality in trying to be independent, but remained a house loving person, loving her family, who came first in everything she did. She and

Edward loved each other's company, and their marriage was well balanced with each of them peppered arguments with good humour, upholding respect and understanding.

'This division of labour Edward dear, that you do this and I do that as you suggested exist only in factories, not in the house. When it comes to the house chores, you don't have to rely on me. You just go and do it, and I'll do the same.'

'Sophie dear there are some chores which are beyond the physical capability of a woman. Will you do them? I guess you won't, this is where I come in.'

Similar arguments didn't aggravate into a heated tit for tat altercation that likely to raise concern. They were both aware of the consequences of continued rebuffs under the same roof. Although not religious, their spiritual self, seemed to have fused somehow into some form of oneness, that they themselves knew how to stay together in sharing the companionship, and affection they cherished for each other.

Forty years had elapsed. Edward and Sophie still enjoyed life together. They lived in Erdington and both retired from their jobs as nurses. Edward still did the odd drawings now and again to keep him occupied, and often came across old staff from Highcroft Hospital on the High Streets of Erdington. Conversations that followed were mainly based on the good old days, and the Hospital, which was undergoing a full revamp to make way for smaller units and housing complex.

Edward, having lived in Erdington for so long, didn't take him much to recognise old friends. His friends on the other hand knew him as soon as they saw him, because despite the coming of old age, his general features were left unaffected. But there was somebody around who had seen him a few times walking up and down the High Streets, and was cautious whether he was the same person who made her cry by the church many moons ago. She was seen a few times looking at him, but didn't dare to approach him, as he gave her an evasive look but a smile after, whenever they passed each other by.

It was 2nd January 2010, that promised a new beginning for some. Edward and Sophie were on the High Street, people around were enthused about what the New Year could bring. Sophie went in one of the 'sales' shops while Edward stood by looking through the window instead. He saw somebody familiar came out, and gave him a smile, and wanted to engage in conversation. It was that woman again: Julie!

'Oh hello, remember me, Julie! I couldn't forget that face you know!'

'Oh Julie, let me think. Oh, how could I forget? I thought I knew you, each time I saw you.'

'After so many years, only your hair had grown grey, Edward.'

'And you Julie still got that blond fringe on your forehead!'

'Oh dear I must be getting younger after so many years… Here is my wife coming out now. Let me introduce you.'

After they had been introduced, Edward told Sophie that he was going to have a chat with Julie before bearing home. And Sophie left them.

They both walked up the High Street, passed the church where they met for the last time. Julie still remembered those drops of tears she shed. Edward still remembered walking away dejected and bruised. But these didn't deter them to want to know more about themselves with the length of time that had branched them off in different directions. Edward invited her for drink, although more relaxed and confident now. He said:

'Let's go for a coffee and talk about it, but not in Edwards Edwards though. This has disappeared for ever!'

'You are still pleasant Edward! We got Greggs in its place now, shall we go there?' said Julie with a smile.

'We can always go there to revive past memories I suppose!'

They both went in Greggs and Edward brought the coffee with some biscuits. They sat on the long bench by the wall, but kept looking at each other.

'There are only some slight changes in you Julie, apart from some wrinkles perhaps which we all could do without. So what you have been doing with yourself then?' asked Edward taking a sip of his coffee.

'Well, I got married to John who wasn't that much good as a husband. Anyway we divorced after ten years. I got a son, married now, and I am a granny. What about you then Edward?'

Edward told her his side of the story. How he found his wife. His son Jim and daughter Tessa had flown the nest. He and Sophie lived on their own with occasional visits from the children who were still single. Although smiling, Edward noticed that she started to become emotional when she asked:

'Have you got any pictures of them on you? I still got the 'hand bag' you gave me you know!'

'No I haven't got their pictures Julie, but nice of you to have kept something 'dear' from the olden days. You retired from work too I presume?'

'Yes I did after ending my career as a midwife at the General Hospital in Worcestershire. I've just moved back to Erdington actually. I lived on my own too, both mum and dad died.'

'Sorry to hear about that.'

She kept looking at Edward and the cup of coffee on the table. Edward noticed her glittering wide eyes suddenly, as she reminisced with a smile:

'You know when I saw you a few times in Erdington, I ask myself why do I want to see you again after those long years, but I sense that there is something in me that is full of regrets, that won't be comforting till I see you. I knew it was all my faults. And that brought me to my weakest, and turned you into a broken man. I still feel sorry about it when I noticed the strength of your feelings. I never knew men could have such emotions till I met you.'

'Oh Julie, please don't bring that up again. It's finished now. I walked away for your own happiness. At first I thought you were my only hope, but, when I realised that you still wanted me after your predicament, I wondered how your husband would take it, because there would be problems. Didn't you love him as much?'

'No I didn't, as he took me for granted, due to the fact we were too closely related I think. We noticed that the love existed as before was no more, even the friendship had vanished. Anyway that's a long story. I couldn't care now he is out of my life. I preferred then to stay single rather than having somebody again like him. I am glad that you have a good life with your wife. I wish I could turn back the clock!'

'Talking about the clock Julie, I remember now you gave me a clock did you? Well, I was so fed up with how things had turned out that I got rid of it. I had wanted 'to fast forward it' in order not to read the same time every day, what was it again, 4 o'clock?'

'You've got a good memory Edward, I respect you for that. This is what helps people to change when they reflect on the past. We all make mistakes. But some people can never learn from them. They don't want to better themselves either. Do you again remember what you said to the girl serving us at Edwards Edwards at the time: 'That time and circumstance may change but human emotions don't?' said Julie smiling.

'I could see you've got a good memory too Julie,' said Edward smiling, 'but remember it's difficult to 'turn back that clock' now. It's only going to cause us more pain. The nostalgic past always haunts us as we grow older. We always search our souls. Sometimes we think it's fate if you believe in the circle of life. Sometimes we think it's our own free will. We can all make decisions about how to live our lives but our interests and desires always come first, irrespective of those that that we think can find their own way around. Because we all become oblivious of what we did at the time, we never realise that how sensible we can become with time. Yes time can be a healer but, emotional pain that is etched on the canvas of our memory no dye in all the world of hues can brush it away. This is the frailty of human nature as our own mind plays tricks upon us just like our eyes!'

Edward noticed Julie's glistening eyes as she stared at her empty cup on the table, and kept her silence. But she suddenly woke up to talk about something different with a smile:

'Do you still draw?'

'Yes, occasionally.'

'You must be very good now, mind you, you were good before. Would you see the same Julie now if you draw me? You could have given me those pictures on your wall at least you know!'

She then continued staring at her cup and said:

'You know we women used to be made to feel that since we could cry, we had to listen for the good advice, and had to submit to the whims and desires of people we depended upon, but not anymore, Edward. I have learned the hard way now with the growing age. But will I still feel for you, I can't tell?'

'I regret things have turned out different for you, Julie, as for me I am happily married, and loved my wife and family.'

Edward hinted that he wouldn't want to get involved again, now that they were both grown up adults. He continued with a smile:

'Sorry I have to go now Julie. Sophie may think I got carried away again. We can always meet for a chat another time. Here is my number on the mobile phone. I am going to walk with you and leave you like I did 40 years ago by the church. Still you haven't told me why you cried so much then?'

'Well my dear Edward, I was crying because I had glimpses of the life ahead, it wouldn't be the same for me without you,' said Julie.

Edward kept his cool, and smiled again. He gave her a kiss on her forehead and they both walked away. Edward reached home after a while. Sophie was waiting for him to have tea. He was intrigued when she said:

'Who was that old woman then?'

'What do you mean, we aren't young either Sophie! That woman happened to be the old girlfriend Julie, 40 years ago, I told you about. It's because of her I found you,' said Edward as he proceeded to give her a kiss.'

'You better keep away from her if you don't want to end up with that witch doctor again, Edward!' said Sophie smiling.

'She looked battered and bruised Sophie. She is living on her own, poor lady. I think she is going to ring me sometimes, but I don't want to get involved anymore!'

'You better don't dearest. You know we search for love from cradle to grave, do you think we will ever find it?' replied Sophie.

'I think I have!' said Edward laughing away.

Sophie started to get worried now about the same woman in his life. Although Edward promised he wouldn't get involved again, she didn't like the idea that Edward wanted to communicate with her in giving her his mobile number. She anxiously said:

'You already told her that you are a happily married man Edward, you don't want to break that happiness do you?'

'No Sophie, no, we just want to stay as friends. Don't you think I had enough of all this romance, and lovey-dovey thing in my old age!

'You don't seem to have enough by the look of it. Well, we shall see.'

A month after there was a call on Edward's phone in the early morning. Sophie took it. Julie was at the other end talking in a shaky voice. She wanted Edward to know that she was diagnosed with breast cancer, and that she was following a treatment regime at the Good Hope Hospital, in Sutton Coldfield. It was a shock for Sophie to hear the news. Edward would feel it more when he heard it. But Sophie kept her cool, didn't know how to tell Edward, as he was still in bed, and it wouldn't be a good idea to wake him up.

Edward got up eventually and inquired:

'Who is that ringing so early Sophie?'

'It wasn't a good morning greeting Edward, I can assure you. It was from your friend Julie again. She had been diagnosed with breast cancer!'

'What! A terrible thing to hear when somebody just got up, I wish it was a dream!'

'No you are not dreaming. It's as dark as the daylight.'

'How come she never told me when I last met her? I wonder why she was holding it back from me. Mind you she looked very down as if in pain at times.'

'And you thought she was still pinning for your love!' said Sophie smiling.

'We can never know, do we? Probably she had it for a long time, suddenly it became worse.'

Edward sat down at the table in his dressing gown, still in shock, sharing cups of tea with Sophie, who sensed his sadness. But she had to carry on with the bad news.

'She is at Good Hope Hospital in the Cancer ward. It appears she is well advanced with it.'

Edward seemed reflective, then continued:

'In this life, the so called happiness and sadness are part of the same coin. I thought she looked great when we met. And I was delighted to listen to what she had to say regarding the olden days. But this wasn't to be now. That coin has been tossed, and sorrow is back facing us. Did she say if her treatment is working, or how long she will be at the Hospital?'

'She just said she didn't have long to live!'

'Oh, what else,' said a dejected Edward. 'Shall we go and visit her later Sophie?'

'Yes we shall Edward. But remember I will only be there like a springboard to provide support for you in case you succumb under the emotional strain. I'm not that enthusiastic about meeting her at all.'

'You've developed a heart of stone Julie.'

'It's all right for you to say that Edward. Remember it's reminiscence about the times, the good times you had with her, when she was young and you were young, she was your muse then, and that corrupted your peace of mind. Now that she is dying and looked different, I wonder if you can accept it. You don't want to return to that old problem of yours again do you?'

'No Sophie I don't, but I would like to see her in her dying days, where a dream is about to be faded.'

Both Sophie and Edward went to visit Julie at the Cancer Unit in Good Hope Hospital that afternoon. Many of her relatives were present at her bedside, including John her ex-husband who was beyond recognition with old age.

Julie was no better either: She was bald and emaciated, but still got some specks of life in her to say her last words to Edward, as she had only half an hour to live. She recognised Edward as she held his hand tight to say: Goodbye Edward.

Julie passed away soon after. When they reached home, a thoughtful and emotional Edward had something to say:

'You know Sophie, the life of an artist never runs smooth. He tries to bring the image of beauty and sorrow to the world. He also suffers the consequence of doing just that. I think the sublimation of feelings has got something to do with it, where his sufferings become works of art. The pictures of her that I burnt a long time ago could be the foreshadowing of her cremation which is going to happen now, for real. I am sad. No Sophie, I won't draw this one!'

Printed in Poland
by Amazon Fulfillment
Poland Sp. z o.o., Wrocław

54573602R00058